Destination - Hell
Torture Magic Novel 4.2 (45)

By Douglas Todt

First Edition (2022)

Destination - Hell
Torture Magic Novel 4.2 (45)

By Douglas Todt

***Destination - Hell**
Torture Magic Novel 4.2 (45)
By Douglas Todt*

This season of Torture Magic is a little different. If you've been a reader of the Outcasts series, you don't have to read the TM series to enjoy the finale, or vice versa. But if you read both, it's more fun.

For readers of the Torture Magic series, series five will be back to the normal format (or close to it) in 2023.

All readers can enjoy the related book, the first appearance of the Cube, Las Vegas' newest superheroine. Shelby's series is set in the Ops world, but it does not *directly* tie-in with the Torture Magic series. Her book I consider 4.X (46) and falls between 4.2 and 4.3 of the regular series.

The Outcasts Path

The Intersection
Outcasts VIII / TM 4.0 "Merger"

Torture Magic Season Four
The Killer Inside (4.1)
Destination - Hell (4.2)
Survival of the Fittest (4.3)
No Ifs, Ands, or Butts (4.4)
The Golden Age (4.5)

Related Books
The Call Girl Superheroine (4X)

Chapter One
Ol' Satan has Visitors

"So, who the fuckity-fuck are these guys anyhow?" asked Satan.

In the ninth circle of Hell, as described by the poet Dante Alighieri in his fourteenth century epic poem *Divine Comedy*, Satan sat on a throne of skulls on a river of solidified lava ringed by volcanoes. This was one of his recreational spots. He stared at a creature that looked like an earthworm that moved by riding on its tail. Upright, it was four feet tall. Hell hosted aliens as well as humans, and this creature, named Gimbly, was a Crustorian from a planet in the distant galaxy of Cigna Minor.[1]

Just take our word for it.

Besides his odd natural appearance, he was wearing a tuxedo jacket, typical form for . . . a butler.

Satan was in one of his more humanoid forms, built like a wrestler and naked, showing off an obscenely large member.

Gimbly handed Satan a binder made of elephant skin that had parchment of the souls of slave-traders. The pages screamed when they were painfully flipped. The binder was huge. "Here's the files."

Satan looked at the binder and made a face as if he'd eaten something rotten. "Look, Dante says this is going to be the final battle for the control of Hell. I have shit to do to get ready. I mean, I like

---

[1] As seen in TM volume 2.2 "Tripper and Geneva – Inferno"

reading, but this is a bit much with all the other shit I gotta do. Can I have the edited highlights? Except for that Nicole Smith chick. You told me about her yesterday."

"Sure, boss."

"Oh, and show me photos. Do you have trading cards? I really like those things."

"I can make some."

"Nah, not right now," he said with a wave of his hand. "Let's just get a rundown. Tripper O'Sullivan and Geneva Kane. Aren't they the two that were here just a while back and got away?"

Gimbly cleared his throat. "Uh, yeah, in '17. There's still people pissed about that, boss."

"Fuck 'em."

"Roger. Okay. Lemme read the bios, boss. Here's what the background guys sent me. I'll just read it verbatim."

"Sounds good, Gimb."

"Tripper is almost 124 years old, a tall man with a cane, a full six feet and six inches tall, looks like someone stretched too fast in a taffy twister. His bones are obvious through his rail-thin frame, but most people didn't notice because he tends to wear bulky clothing — jeans and a white T-shirt stained with mustard. He sports a mop of unruly, uncombed black hair buried under a ratty Atlanta Braves baseball cap, an untrimmed black beard, and dark-rimmed black glasses typical of the military — function over fashion. His wooden cane is carved into the shape of the head of a cottonmouth snake, and these days is mostly for show. The flask it holds occasionally helps channel a spell, but the cane is primarily to help channel his unique form of geometric channeling. Besides that, it throws opponents off guard, giving him the element of surprise in combat.

"Tripper's lived a very long life due to an Infusion of zombie magic from a necromancer, Phineas Trout, when Tripper was a teenager."

"Hey, isn't he the guy that got demoted to the maggot pits for failing when Tripper was here last time?"

"Yeah, that's him. Boy, he and his wife sure did scream about that. Until we ripped out their tongues. Anyhow, back to Tripper. See, his long life is not just zombie magic, it's mostly psychological. As a teen, he'd abandoned his best and only friend, fellow adolescent Caroline, to be raped and murdered by a gang. He ran. Her death meant he knew he'd go to Hell. But after escaping Hell in '17 and, stopping Caroline's spirit, which made it out as well, he's reached a certain peace with his past."

Satan chuckled. "Well, we'll ruin that peace for sure! Okay, Kane."

"Ah. She's the heavy-hitter of this team. Thirty-three-year-old Ops paranormal agent Geneva Kane is a pretty woman, one that has matured considerably from the snotty teenager that joined Ops when she was just eighteen. Now she's a mature, attractive, *classy* woman, although not exceptionally beautiful. She has wavy black hair that is straight on top with bangs in front. Her hair is draped halfway down her shoulders. Her eyes are bright blue and her face slightly square shaped but attractive. Her smile is cute and occasionally sassy. Her body is not as shapely as some, but she's attractive, with lots of curves, especially her bottom, legs and hips. She's a proper weight for her five-and-one-half-foot frame, but not in great shape — she despises working out but is good with her diet."

"I'm not interested in her diet," muttered Satan.

"Sorry. Uh, anyhow, she spends a lot of time visiting her mother, who is spending most of her time these days at Geneva's grandparents' old home, a historical lighthouse. They're working on a contracting bid to restore some of the buildings on the property."

"The grandparents . . . isn't Gerald one of those guys that bitch-slapped Hitler in '45? I'm sure I've heard that name in his endless whining about losing that battle."

"Yeah, boss. Good memory. Geneva's grandparents Gerald and Mary, both deceased now, were her best friends as a child. Gerald taught Geneva channeling after she manifested when sixteen to rescue her dog from drowning in the Atlantic, showing her first signs of her considerable elemental channeling ability. Gerald died in 2015 helping the team attempt to stop Elkrod's takeover of Atlantia"

"Oh, that's right. That's what did in ol' Doc Voodoo eventually, right?"

"Yep."

Satan rubbed his chin. "Ol' Doc is still on the downlow after that fiasco, isn't he?"

"Yep."

"Okay, Geneva, she's pretty and classy. So what?"

"Her channeling is the thing. She's a level-one elemental channeler, so good at channeling she can even use TK on normal objects. But she has a lot of other shit going on. For one thing, she's got affinity to the probability cloud."

"Those are those things that alter probability due to a quantum tachyon field, right? They make the improbable slightly less improbable."

"Yeah. Boss, who the fuck explained a quantum tachyon field to you?"

"Hey, I have other assistants. Keep going."

"Sure. Well, back before Christmas, Geneva was fighting this woman named Calico Kelkirk. Geneva got dumped into a chamber and was hit with a tachyonic surge of undefined origin. Her powers jumped up on a quantum level. She can actually change matter, but it isn't fully under her control and isn't fully clear what is actually happening."

"Hmmmmmm . . . don't like the unknown."

"It does make her a wildcard."

"Ah, Gimb, c'mon. Y'know channeling doesn't follow Earth rules here. Everything is in the mind."

"That just makes her *more* dangerous. There's not a mentally tougher or more confident woman alive. Uh, so to speak."

Satan pondered that, rubbing his chin. "Okay, point taken. Boy, you're a pain in the ass, always gotta be right. Next up."

"Well, the semi leader is Sylvester Starnes, the Immortal Man."

"Oh, him! Lay it on me, man."

"Sylvester has one of those handsome, chiseled faces, dark brown eyes, and gray hair, the sort of man that defines distinguished. At six-foot three and 225, he is also well built physically. His body is covered in scars, a legacy of being immortal but not invulnerable."

"Ouch."

"No shit. Anyhow, in 1776, at the age of twenty-three, he picked the wrong victim and was caught by a witch named Deliah. She cursed him, made him immortal, and removed his ability to channel TM. Since then, he largely wandered, only occasionally taking an interest in human affairs . . . at least until 2014, when he took over Special Operations when General Jameson was fired.

"Few in Ops trusted him his first few years as director. The Director of Field Ops, Sam Grant, thought Sylvester was a dog on a leash, and that if the leash were removed, he'd be a biter, so to speak. But Sylvester proved his attempts to change were grounded in who he was as a man, not the curse, when he fought off Everett in his attempt to save Meredith Patience.

"Sylvester was the one to put Little Jack in charge, and the operations now run smoothly. Grant's in a coma now anyhow, has been since the team battled this freak-ass alien called Quotient on New Year's Day."

Satan waved his hand. "Ah, I know about the Horal. Skip them for now. Who is this last one?"

"Carole Kress. She's the one that is the most . . . and in some ways least . . . important."

"Gonna have to explain that one, Gimb."

"I figured as much," said Gimbly, and he sighed. "Kress is a torture magician, one that uses the adrenaline and aural energy from torture to convert to energy to engage in telekinesis. As I'm sure you know. Anyhow, now forty-three, she looks in her mid-twenties with obviously colored, fire-red hair that is cut short and wavy, blue eyes, perfect teeth, and a fine profile. Her figure is lithe but endowed, and her arms are oddly a little long for her body. Now, she's one of those really rare types of paranormal. You know, like telepaths and soul survivors. She's a portal crucible."

"Yeah, that rings a bell. She's a walking portal, right?"

"Yep. She's covered in brands. They are all shapes and sizes and cover her entire body. Some are figures, some are pictures, some are symbols, some are numbers and letters, and some were geometric shapes. They vary in size. Because of the brands, her skin isn't even. It is as lumpy and varied as the southern California topography. The only areas spared the brands are her neck upwards and her hands from the wrist out — if she wears long sleeves and high-collared shirts, the brands aren't observable. She was a torture magician for some years, but apparently gave it up."

"Yeah, yeah, I've heard of this. A few beings have been down here can do that. They zap right out. Pain in the ass."

"She also knows of the Horal."

Satan's eyes lit up. "Oh, now I get it! These candy-asses think they can come down here and stop the Horal?"

"What I gather from Dante is the Horal are an alien race, and they plan to imprison them in Hell because Hell is purely a construct of the human mind . . . or humanoid mind. After all, we know a human created the place with the blank-slate gem."

"Yeah," said Satan, rubbing his chin. "Who devised this plan?"

"That's a guy named Sam Grant, who led a battle against Quotient, one of the Horal."

"Interesting, interesting," muttered Satan, still rubbing his chin. "Y'know, sometimes in these conflicts, it's best to stay neutral and side with the winner."

"I don't know if that's an option. I could ask Virgil. Ever since Dante took over chronicling, Virgil feels a bit left out."

"Nah. So, did Sam send this team here?"

"His subconscious did. He's in a coma."

"Now, that's fascinating," said Satan with a chuckle. "Then where does Smith fit in?

"I don't know. You're the boss. You figure it out."

Satan glared. "Don't get pissy, Gimb. So, we have these four."

"Yes."

"It seems to me that they have specific reasons to be here. Kress to get them here. Tripper and Geneva have been here and are very powerful. And Starnes, he's immortal . . . I suspect Sam has a special plan for him."

"I'd bet on it."

"Where does Smith fit in? I mean, she's just a girl. For God's sake, she's a fucking actress. A theatre actress, granted, but just an actress. Mom got sick and died, dad poisoned, best friend died when she was 20, rare disease, nothing important here."

"You're forgetting her abilities and the repressed memory in her file."

Satan's eyes lit up again. "Oh, that memory is gonna get dealt with *here*?"

"Yeah. There's agents from heaven crawling all over the place. I've told you, this is big shit. Dante doesn't chronicle your everyday ball game."

"Ah, there's agents from Heaven here all the time. They're worse than homeless people in San Francisco."

"Not people like *these*." Gimbly handed him a list.

"Whoa! You're right . . . y'know, the more I think about this, the more I like the idea of laying low."

"You're the boss."

"Yeah . . . yeah, we're just going to lay low and watch the show."

Chapter Two
Ambushed. Well, of Course!

"Y'all'd think wakin' up dead would be easier on the joints," muttered Tripper as he slowly pushed himself up with both hands. Once he got to his knees, he looked around to confirm all his partners had made the journey to Hell with him.

They had . . . well, almost. He immediately realized they weren't *quite* in Hell. They were on a rocky basin that looked like a dock at a pier, but this dock led to a river of blood that was the River Styx.

Waiting for them in a small canoe was Charon, the ferryman who would take them across the river into Hell. Charon was a tall, emaciated man with white hair and beard, and more unpleasantly, empty eye sockets with fire ants crawling in and out of them. He wore a black cloak and looked like an anorexic Santa Claus. He held an oar in his left hand and pointed at Tripper with the right.

"Come ye aboard?"

"In a sec, old-timer," said Tripper, scrambling to look around at his team.

Nicole Smith, Carole Kress, Geneva Kane, and Sylvester Starnes were all coming around. Tripper noted with satisfaction all were dressed in Hell as they had been on Earth, wearing gray Kevlar to help if there were feedback in the form of psychic heat, meaning they still had control of their auras, their souls. Tripper even had his cottonmouth snake shaped cane, which he used to get to his feet.

He immediately aided Geneva, who shook her head and said, "That was some trip."

"I know, reckon y'all gotta get with it fast. Can you remember our '17 trip now?"

Geneva frowned. "I . . . I think . . . I do . . . it's coming back in a rush."

"I thought we weren't supposed to remember," said Tripper, getting Geneva fully to her feet. He noticed Sylvester was quickly up and about, helping Kress and Nicole to their feet.

Geneva furrowed her brow and said, "That was my . . . understanding. That it was to protect ourselves. But maybe it was . . . some effect of portaling?"

"I dunno, but with our memories back . . . it could get rough."

She frowned. "It's not like that. It's like a comic book. I remember what happened, but I'm not emotionally involved."

"Comic book?" asked Tripper, taking off his hat and scratching his head.

"Well, like stuff my gramps would draw in his comic books that had the Black Flashlight. No, more like we were avatars in a computer game. We did all the steps, but the emotional impact seems . . . muted."

"Could be. I knew a fella in the Big One," he said, referring to World War II, "who remembered the whole war in shades of brown. Everything was the color of dirt. Mind is a great thing."

"Well, let's not stick around here and study it," said Geneva irritably. "We've a job to do."

"Reckon so," said Tripper.

Sylvester approached, Nicole and Kress slightly behind them. Kress was popping her neck. Nicole looked confused, while Sylvester looked concerned as he said, "We must ride the Styx."

Nicole looked around. Twenty-four-years-old, she wasn't extraordinarily pretty, but she was attractive. Average height and weight, her main asset was her face, which had the profile of a model. Her lips were ruby red, her skin fair and perfect, her eyes a brilliant shade of bright blue. Her hair was long, wavy, and jet black, running over her shoulders and down her back, with wide-cut bangs that ended just above her eyebrows in front.

Her voice was sometimes soft and sometimes throaty. As a stage actress, she knew how to change her appearance and manner to get her point across. Physically, she stayed in shape with CrossFit workouts, but often she did them at home online. And while her features were average, she knew how to accent them to make them appear more favorable.

The atmosphere smelled of sulfur and cat pee, the rocks were hot, and the sky was red. Screams echoed as if they were in a Halloween haunted house.

"This . . . is a little over my head," said Nicole worriedly.

"Shit, it's over all our heads, young'n. Just hang tight," said Tripper, patting her shoulder in a fatherly manner.

Kress stopped popping her neck and looked around. "This place could use a makeover."

"We're not here to love it or list it," muttered Geneva. "We're here to stop the Horal."

Sylvester nodded towards Charon. "We're not quite in Hell yet. We must cross the river. Charon will have to take us across."

Charon looked at them and smiled.

Nicole made a face. "That's creepy. It's like looking at Death having an orgasm."

Tripper laughed. "I like y'all."

Nicole blew him a kiss. "If only you were under one-hundred."

"Enough," said Sylvester, clearly edgy. "Let us advance. The war begins now."

Tripper and Geneva exchanged looks. Nicole nodded, following Sylvester as he led the party. Kress continued to look around.

Suddenly, a creature that looked like an earthworm but with one large eye and a mouth moved in front of them. It was six feet tall and wearing a tuxedo. He had a sign tied around his torso that read:

PASSAGE REQUIRES TICKET

Sylvester glared at the creature. "Who are you, creature?"

"I'm Sid. Sid Shores, known as Wombo by the home-boys on the planet Sykorak. I killed forty-six worm boys in my time. Who the fuck are you, white-face?"

His voice dark, Sylvester glared and said, "The Immortal Man."

Sid said, "Hmpf. I've heard of you. Got a ticket?"

"We wish to cross," said Sylvester, and he moved to advance. But an invisible barrier stopped him at the edge of the rock, just a foot short of the canoe-shaped ferry. This close, Sylvester could see it was made of bone and covered in rotting human flesh that was inundated with flies.

Chopin's funeral march began to play.

"Even you need a ticket," said Sid, almost apologetically.

Nicole looked at Kress, thought about asking her a question, then turned to Geneva. "Uh, he's an alien?"

Geneva nodded. "Aliens and animals go to Hell as well. It's a blank slate dimension. Your own subconscious thoughts pull you here."

"Damn. If I run into a homicidal cow, I'm leaving," said Nicole, making a comment reflecting astonishment more than an actual threat or joke.

Tripper moved forward, stopping Sylvester, who looked like he might be about to punch out Sid. Tripper said, "Wombo, as the home-boys call you, how do we get a ticket?"

Sid snickered. "I can probably hook you up. But I gotta be entertained. I've been in Hell for like five thousand years now. I'm pretty fuckin' bored. How about we have one of the girl toys here give a horse a blow job?"

They all looked at Kress. She gave them the finger.

"You?" Sid asked, turning to Geneva.

"I'm married," she said, artfully dodging the request with grace.

"Ah." He looked at Nicole. "You . . . you might enjoy it too much."

Nicole flushed with rage and embarrassment. "You maggot. How dare you insinuate that?"

She moved forward to slug him, but Sylvester stopped her with an arm-bar.

"I call 'em like I see 'em. Anyhow, we don't seem to be getting anywhere."

Tripper looked at Geneva. "We gotta be in Hell already. Bureaucracy like this can only come from Satan."

Sid laughed. "Aw, I'm just pullin' your legs. Is that what they say up there these days? We do try ta stay contemporary down here. There's nothing worse than being a dated old fuck."

"If you mean you're pulling a practical joke, yes, we still say that," said Geneva, making it clear she was not at all amused by the joke.

Sylvester added, "So we may, without adversity, advance?"

"Oh, sure. I was just waiting for your chronicler to show up."

"Chronicler?" asked Nicole. "I don't think that's a real word."

"Actually, it is, dumb-ass. Man, I can tell you went to USC. It's a person who writes about great historical events, and he's here now."

Sid nodded, and the five turned to look at the man approaching from an incongruously placed bus made of bones that had stopped at a bus stop constructed from the intestines of giant whales.

Brow furrowed, Geneva said, "You look familiar."

He was a handsome man with curly brown hair, light blue eyes, a masculine jaw, and a well-built body despite being taller than normal. He wore a black suit with a yellow tie, the jacket unbuttoned. Geneva noticed it immediately as a designer suit, and therefore very expensive.

"Y'all look kind'a like Dan Marino in his better days," said Tripper.

The man chuckled. "That comment has been made before."

Suddenly, Geneva's eyes widened, and she snapped her fingers and pointed at him as if she were a starstruck teen meeting a movie star. "*Dante*! Dante!"

"Now you remember," he said with a wink.

Geneva ran to him and hugged him, laughing. "I can't believe it! How did you — why are you here *now*?"

Suddenly serious, Dante said, "I've always been here, Geneva."

Confused, Geneva said, "You don't remember our escape in '17? Has it been that long?"

Dante shook his head. "No, you misunderstand. You *never* met me before, Miss Kane."

Taken aback, Geneva took . . . a step back. "I . . . I did. You told me Tripper loved me . . . helped us escape."

Dante shook his head, looking as sad as a tired hound. "You didn't meet me. I don't reside in Hell, Miss Kane."

"Geneva, please."

"Geneva. I work with the angels, trying to warn people about Hell, trying to help them escape while they are still on Earth, to repent. As a chronicler, I also record momentous events. You couldn't have met me. No offense, but your previous arrival wasn't that big of a deal."

Pondering this for a moment, Geneva said, "I should've suspected. Hell is, after all, the land of lies."

"I'm sorry."

"Then . . . then who *did* I meet?"

Dante shrugged. "I don't know. Nor is it important."

But for Geneva, it was *hugely* important, for it was this conversation that made her realize she loved Tripper . . . a love that he never reciprocated, a love she abandoned eventually for her now husband Lon. But if that was all a sham . . . then she had been cruelly manipulated, played by a master of emotional torment.

And that *royally* pissed her off.

Geneva said coldly, "I *will* find out one day."

Dante cleared his throat and said, "Ah, well, that is for another time."

Nicole stepped forward and said, "Wait. You said you record momentous events. This is one of them?"

"The pursuit of the Horal is unparalleled in human history." Dante looked at Sylvester. "Surely *you* understand that."

Sylvester stared and nodded once, slowly.

"Then should we get on with it?" asked Kress, clearly irritated.

"Yes," said Dante. "I will sign for the ticket, Sid, and then we can go for a ride upstream."

"Y'all make it sound like we're goin' river rafting," muttered Tripper. He opened the head of his cane and found a vial of moonshine. He downed it, shook his head, and said, "That clears out the old sinuses. I can die happy how. Let's roll."

Kress kept looking around nervously. She was the last one to board the canoe. Tripper and Geneva sat on one side, Geneva on his left. On the other, Sylvester and Nicole sat, Nicole on his left. Kress remained standing in the rear with Dante. Once they were aboard, Charon pushed off, using an oar of cow bones.

"Have fun, kids," said Sid.

Once they were sailing on the river of blood, they moved slowly but steadily. The sound of exploding volcanoes became louder.

Kress continued to look around constantly, especially staring at the sky. Nicole finally said, "Stop it, Kress. You're getting on my nerves. You act like Freddie Kruger is about to jump out of the closet."

"Fucking idiot. It's worse than that," she said, clearly scared.

Nicole looked at Sylvester. "If she's cracking up already, we're in big trouble."

Sylvester stared at Charon, then looked at Nicole. "She'll be fine."

Tripper said, "Well, I reckon so. But even if the Horal ain't after us, we ain't exactly gonna be voted the most popular down here. I done sent half these sumbitches down here in the Big One, and I imagine y'all sent a few down here back in the day as well."

"Yes," said Sylvester, surprisingly without elaboration.

Geneva looked at Dante. "Are the Voodoos here? Did Andrea come back here after we destroyed her host body? What about Doc Voodoo?"

"They're all keeping a very low profile these days. The whole thing in '17 cost them seriously. They are no longer considered major players in Hell."

"I guess I should be happy, but I'd more say I'm relieved," said Geneva. "Is this a long ride? We're kind of sitting ducks out here."

Dante spoke. "We're safe on the river. None can attack before we enter Hell."

Those words went under the category of "Famous Last."

Just moments after Dante spoke, the ferry was suddenly launched into the air by an attack from below by the largest whale any of them had ever seen. It's existence in the river of blood was illogical, but then, all of Hell defied most physics because it was a construct of the subconscious of man and the other creatures inhabiting the realm.

"Abandon ship!" shouted Dante, and all of them followed his lead as he dove like an Olympic swimmer into the blood.

Charon remained on the ferry, which split in half. Charon inexplicably 'surfed' on his piece of the ferry, riding it down to the bloody river. There he gestured and instantly recreated the now missing second half. The original second half sank to the bottom of the river.

Tripper grabbed Geneva and said, "It's an attack!"

"Well, no kidding," said Geneva, making a face.

Sylvester swam for the shore, Nicole right behind him.

Kress remained in place, paddling, looking confused and horrified at being in a river of blood.

Dante moved to help her.

As he did so, they heard a horrific sound, as if thousands of Aztec warriors were erupting from the jungle to slaughter them in their sleep, as if all the nightmares of man were combined into one, as if a tornado were screaming.

Kress screamed.

Tripper and Geneva looked at each other in horror.

Sylvester stopped swimming and treaded blood. Nicole did the same, then looked at him.

"What is it?"

But she never got an answer. Because at that moment, Kress stopped screaming and shouted, "They're ripping me aparttttttttttttttt!"

She vanished.

Seconds later . . . they *all* vanished.

Chapter Three
Tripper, Geneva, and the Pig Boy

"Uhhhhhhhhhhhhhhh . . . where am I?" moaned Geneva as she awakened and saw, to her shock, a clear blue sky worthy of the best summer days in Maine.

Slowly, she rolled to her right side and asked, "Am I *home*?"

Then she heard Tripper moan. As her vision cleared, she saw Tripper on his back a few yards away. Studying her surroundings, she realized they were on the rim of a volcanic crater. The rocks were reddish ash mixed with a few large boulders and trees that had been snapped at the base and burned . . . it looked like Mount Saint Helens, where she had fought David Mize's avatar, the TM Everett, in 2018.

Tripper was waking up. Geneva forced herself to her knees. They were on the upper rim. In the bowl of the volcano, which oddly had stairs of ash leading down, there was a large red and white house with a large sign in cartoonish fashion in front labeled, "Information."

"Weird," said Geneva. She realized the sky above the crater was blue, but it was purplish and red to the sides. Additionally, in the distance she could hear the rumbles of thunder and the screams of the damned that were as typical background noise in Hell as the sound of airplanes at O'Hare. And while it was warm but not uncomfortable in the bowl, every time she felt a breeze it was like a blast from an industrial furnace.

"Gol' damn drunk drivers," muttered Tripper, slowly awakening and rolling to his left. His cane lay to his side, and he picked it up.

"Tripper, can you hear me?" asked Geneva, stumbling to his side and helping him to his feet.

"Yeah . . . what the Hell happened? Reckon that Moby Dick shit wasn't in the plan."

"I'd guess not."

"Where are we?"

"I'm . . . not sure," she said, looking around, her voice soft with worry and awe. "I suspect we're somewhere in Hell, but this little cone of the volcano seems almost like Earth."

Tripper took in his surroundings, then pointed at the building with his cane. "Place looks like a tollbooth in Denmark. Let's go check it out. Ain't nothin' else around here anyways."

"Agreed."

As they started to walk, Geneva began to hum a tune. Primed for the battle of his life, this highly annoyed Tripper and he snapped, "What in tarnation are you singin' for, Kane?"

She shrugged. "I don't know."

"What is it, anyhow? Y'all ain't the best at carrying a tune."

Putting on a pout, Geneva said, "It's *I Got a Name* by Jim Croce."

"Well, hearing you hum it probably has him turning in his grave."

Ignoring his critique, she said, "He died too young." Then she continued to hum the tune.

"That is really getting on my nerves."

"Well, it's helpful," said Geneva slyly. "Anything that is anti-Hell helps us keep our own personalities. Ultimately, Hell isn't about physical punishment. It's about breaking the will and destroying the soul."

"Ain't no song in the world gonna stop that."

"It helps. Besides, I carry a tune just fine," she said with a sassy swing of her hip.

"Real music is Johnny Cash . . . actually, that ain't true. The best musician I ever heard was a guy named Ralph Carpenter. He was a traveling salesman from Memphis I ran into back in the days when I ran with Jude and Nate as my posse."

"Back in the twenties, right?"

"More or less. Anyhow, we went into a speak-easy one night and he mesmerized the crowd. Reckon he was some type of channeler. I ain't never heard music like that . . . there ain't music like that."

"What happened to him? I've never heard of him," said Geneva.

"He died six months later from pneumonia." Tripper shook his head. "Reckon many die too soon . . . when you're 120-ish, *everyone* dies too soon."

Geneva nodded and said, "It must make you very lonely."

"Ya gets used to it."

Geneva doubted that, but she didn't press the point because they were almost to their destination, the walk to the information booth taking only ten minutes. They were both silent now, trying to absorb what was happening and worried about Nicole, Kress, Dante, and Sylvester. They had expected this to be a difficult mission, but they had already gotten off to a more difficult start than anticipated.

At the booth, they saw it was ringed by a bone, picket fence and plastic daffodils. A window was cut out of the booth, just like an information booth at a county fair, and inside was a man that was . . . well, a pig. Not messy, but an actual porcine — or more accurately, if a pig evolved into a man, that would be this man. He wore a brown suit, yellow tie, and old-style spectacles. Busy studying a huge book with a blue cover and Greek words, he put it aside, folded his hands on the tiny shelf that made the bottom of the window, and said, "Miss Kane, Mr. O'Sullivan, I'm Porker. Glad to help."

They shook hands. His hand was hot and wet. "Uh, pleased," said Geneva.

"Information, huh? What kind'a Hell-trap is this?" asked Sullivan, rubbing his beard.

Waving his hands in shock at being accused, Porker said, "No, no, no! You have it all wrong. This is the information booth for Hell. We're technically not part of Hell. We simply assume the native lands of the life-form that was, ah, dispatched from the ferry."

Geneva frowned. She knew Hell was also the home of aliens and animals, so given their environment, what he said made sense. Granted, Mount Saint Helens wasn't the nicest place on Earth, but it was Earth. However, his last words caught her ear. "Dispatch? We were attacked, the ferry ripped apart — something we believed was off limits."

Porker snorted and chuckled, a very unpleasant sound. Tripper and Geneva looked at each other. Tripper then said to him, "Something funny, bacon boy?"

The screams were now louder in the distance. Porker pushed his spectacles up his snout and said, "There are no rules in Hell other than those made by the leaders. Well, I take that back. There are rules." He began ticking them off his porcine fingers. "God can't be harmed. His agents can't be harmed. The living can't be retained if they resist."

"I know that," said Geneva smugly.

"And everyone else is fair game."

"So why did we wind up here when the boat capsized?" asked Geneva.

"Ferry. You two are unique. Like Dante, you entered Hell alive and escaped."

"Our partners are the same, and they aren't with us," said Geneva.

Porker shrugged. "What do I know? Don't know *why* you're here and they aren't. I do know that few people ever, ever, ever come back like you two! *Why* are you here?" he asked, seemingly genuinely curious.

"To trap the Horal in Hell and save the Earth," said Geneva.

Porker studied her. "Hmmmmmmm. Well, okay then."

"Y'all seem a bit skeptical," said Tripper, jutting his head forward and slamming his cane on the shelf. "I'm already a mite tired of your attitude and sure could go for some sausage patties."

"Oh, stop it, Trip, he's cute," said Geneva, rubbing his hand. "Do you know where in Hell our friends are?"

"In various areas of torment in Hell. They were claimed by those here. But you two cannot be claimed. Because of your past escape, you're immune."

"Immune?" asked Geneva. "Define that."

"No one can instigate Hell on you. Unless you fall prey to your own guilt, you're safe," said Porker, and with a sinister smile he glared at Tripper, who had begun to sweat.

"So how do we find 'em?" asked Tripper, spitting.

"You don't. They'll either escape, as being alive they have that potential, or they will fall prey and join the billions here already. Meanwhile, you two might as well continue your mission. I'd avoid the upper levels. If you want to trap these Horal, you'll need to use the full blank dimension capabilities, and that is always held by whoever holds the power in the ninth circle — which isn't Satan these days. He still lives there, but he ain't in charge. Ever since old Dante got his name around, he's lost some power. Vlad the Impaler had that area for a couple centuries, but the last century or so, It's been a decade by decade battle. It's, what would you call it, a job with a high turnover ratio."

"Reckon so. Who all is down there, besides ol' horny?" asked Tripper, making devil horns with his fingers, referring to Satan.

"The one who is making all the waves these days, is making his move on ol' Satan's seat . . . is Hitler."

Tripper's face went cold. Geneva knew why. Tripper had been part of the team that included Gerald Kane, Geneva's late grandfather, that had stopped Hitler at the end of World War II. Hitler hadn't committed suicide in his bunker. Several paranormals had killed him, for he was the greatest TM of his time . . . perhaps of all time.

"How do we find him?" said Tripper grimly, grabbing Porker by the trim on his shirt.

"Easy! You gotta work your way to him."

"Work?" asked Geneva, not sure of his meaning in this context.

Porker rubbed his chin. "Well, see, since you two are alive, you're on a bit of a . . . work exemption."

"We were livin' when we got zapped here before and we didn't have no work requirement," said Tripper ruefully.

"Yeah, but that was different. Before, Blue Square sent you here via a tachyon dimensional portal that put you in a blank dimension that was *absorbed* by Hell. You were alive, true, but *technically* part of the merger. *Legally*, you were owned by Hell. But because you were alive, your minds fought off the conditioning and you escaped."

"So Hell really *is* Hell, that stuff about Hell consuming other dimensions and growing, everything Andrea said was true?" asked Geneva, her eyes alight with triumph. She had always been convinced this was true Hell, and this seemed proof.

"Yes, but again, being alive, you were in the outer reaches . . . it's hard to explain," he said, scratching his head.

"Okay, whatever," said Tripper with annoyance. "This ain't getting us any closer to closing the score with Hitler or finding the Horal, for that matter. Reckon y'all is information, so inform us, bacon bits. How do we find our way around?"

Puling pamphlets from behind his booth, he smiled and said, "I can sell you a map for only a tenth of your soul!"

Tripper reached across and bobbed him on the nose.

"Owwwwwwwwww!"

Tripper took the map and then handed a second one to Geneva as he told Porker, "I ain't no tourist, ya ugly pig-man."

Geneva looked at the map. "Tripper, it's basically blank."

Holding his nose, Porker said, "You have to visualize what you want, and it will materialize on the map." He glared at Tripper. "It requires brain power and concentration." He laughed and pointed at Geneva. "You'll probably have to do the work, cutie."

"You tried to sell us a map we create with our *own* thoughts?" asked Geneva with dripping disappointment at his con-man mentality.

"Hey, even a pig has to make a buck."

Geneva looked at Tripper. "I had always thought animals were more innocent than humans, that they lacked the ability to make consciously evil choices. Guess I was wrong."

"Reckon so. Let's roll. We got work to do if'n we're gonna find the others." He frowned and took off his hat, wiped his brow of sweat, and put the hat back on. "In fact, maybe we need some partners."

"Partners?" she asked with obvious surprise.

"Yeah." He snapped his fingers. "We gotta find Krissy McKnight. I remember her from before, and I'm sure she's still here."

"Okay, sure." She studied the map and frowned.

"What y'all thinking about?" asked Tripper, because she stopped moving and stood still.

"Just concerned about . . . *others* that might be here."

Tripper nodded. Before he could comment, however, the map began to glow with red dots and names of those Geneva thought about. As the map began to form, Parker and the tollbooth vanished, replaced by a chariot made of bone that was coated in ice.

Geneva looked at Tripper with a frown. He shook his head and used his cane to point at the chariot. "Reckon someone's got plans for us."

"But who? Hitler? Elkrod? Quafara? Hell, even Gary Hart? We have a lot of enemies — shocking for people as nice as we are," she said, making a rare joke in a time of crisis.

"Yeah. Every sumbitch we crossed done made his way down here," he said darkly.

Geneva looked at the map, nodding. Then she gasped.

"What's wrong?"

One name suddenly jumped out at Geneva, and she said coldly, "He's here now, no surprise."

Tripper said, "Who's that?"

"Mize."

Tripper nodded. David Mize was a TM who took advantage of the probability cloud created when Zenith destroyed Ops' underground research complex in Arizona, unleashing the alien known as Subject Six and imbuing Jennifer Saunders with her unique channeling abilities in 2004. In 2006, Mize built a complex machine using Geneva as a captive to power it, trying to harness the powers. Geneva escaped and, with Jen's help, put pay to his plan.

Most thought Mize died in 2014 in combat with Meredith Patience in the California desert. But he survived, though in a coma. His avatar, a man named Everett, was purely a manifestation of Mize's subconscious and sought to kill Meredith. Geneva's subconscious finally killed Mize's subconscious in battle in a mental toy store.

Ops had some weird battles.

Geneva despised Mize. Her captivity at his hands for several days in '06 still grated after all these years. Being helpless did not sit well with her. Mize disgusted her.

Tripper knew this and said, "Reckon we all gotta focus, Kane. We're here to stop the Horal. Right?"

"Right."

"If Porker was telling the truth, we gotta stop Hitler to get the power to stop the Horal."

Geneva got into the passenger side of the chariot cautiously, avoiding pools of bile and blood, and said, "Why would we believe Porker?"

Tripper rubbed his chin through his beard and also entered, which was much more difficult for him. He was long and spider-shaped, while the chariot was tiny and built much more for someone Geneva's size.

"Reckon that's the most sensible question ever, given Hell is a place of lies. But there's rules here. We learned that the first time. Hell is a place of fiefdoms."

Geneva studied him. "I don't see how that helps, and I also don't know how we drive this thing."

"Reckon we just think, and it will take us. Lemme focus on Krissy a'fore I answer your other question."

"Okay."

Tripper shut his eyes and concentrated, and the chariot began to roll. They moved along the side of the volcano towards what looked like a city made of buildings constructed of black glass, but on closer inspection were really black volcanic rock. There were streets, flooded with blood and littered with body parts; not just human, but also animal and alien.

"Reckon we should be close," said Tripper after a time, shielding his eyes from the brutally hot Hell sun.

"Who is Krissy exactly?" asked Geneva.

"She's a gal pal I met back in '68 when I first ran across that sumbitch Blue Square, down in Cape Canaveral," said Tripper.

Geneva said, "I read about that in Ops' case files, and Golden Bear had Lexx's files on it, but I don't recall much detail related to that case," said Geneva thoughtfully. She also paused and mentally changed clothes, now wearing black yoga pants with brown pirate boots for extra foot protection, and a pillowing yellow blouse with a black belt for a dash of color.

Tripper turned and said, "Is this really th' time to be playin' dress up, Kane?"

"Standards are important even in Hell. Perhaps even more so here." She pointed at her head. "It's all here. The right approach is important."

Tripper rolled his eyes. "Women and clothes. Ain't never understood it."

"*That's* not a surprise," she said dryly.

For a moment, she remembered being in love with him after their return from Hell . . . it seemed a million years ago, and now she wondered how that had *ever* happened. But if course, she now knew she had been pushed towards it by two factors: the trauma of being alone in Hell and the push from whoever had been disguised as Dante.

Still . . . it seemed like some *other* person that had been in love with him, not her. Had she matured? Was she still somewhat 'under the influence' of Hell back in '17? She didn't know . . . and ultimately it didn't matter.

As they approached a clearing in the forest, Geneva asked, "So is Krissy a paranormal?"

"Nope. She was a secretary at the base, at Canaveral. She helped me find the lovers' lane where what's-his-name and his people were using Blue Square to set up some kind of geometric channeling — which killed the victims. I think one made it. Dunno. Hard to remember after all these years . . . shit, I been in battles that poets would sing about that I don't even remember any more."

With mock sympathy, Geneva said, "You must be getting very old."

"Aw, wait until your ass gets flabby and your tits sag, smart-ass."

She laughed, despite their dire surroundings. When she had been a young woman teamed with Tripper and Colin, such comments sounded insulting to her, an expression of male chauvinism designed to keep them in charge. But she had learned over her many, many years working off-and-on with Tripper that he was a typical Southern male in one respect —: talking about feelings was forbidden. His crass jokes and abrasive nature kept away most people and protected him from having to talk about his feelings. That wasn't unusual in men, was more common in men from the South, and certainly was more common of men born during Tripper's era.

Understanding his nature, such comments were no longer . . . crass. And she was glad about that. It made life much more enjoyable.

The chariot suddenly paused. A sign at the end of the city road, which was also the end of the city as it buttressed a gigantic crystal wall that seemed to stretch up to the infinite, was painted on bone in blood. The sign read:

NASA. WE DON'T HAVE PROBLEMS.

"I guess this is the place?" asked Geneva with hesitation.

"Yep. Uh, anyhow, while this thing parks, what I was getting at was Hell is a construct of human minds, so it's gotta have some type of human organization."

"True. Logically, that means the patterns that we have while alive exist here as well," said Geneva thoughtfully.

The bone chariot parked outside a building with no windows and a steel door hewn into the volcanic rock. The only item outside was a sign painted in human fat that read:

ASYLUM.

"Reckon this is it," said Tripper, awkwardly exiting the chariot. Geneva popped out like a piece of toast in a toaster.

"Trip . . . are you here because Krissy can help, or you trying to just help her escape?"

"Reckon a bit of both."

"Are you sure about this?" asked Geneva, clearly anxious.

"Yeah. I owe her. I'll explain later."

They entered and found themselves facing rows and rows of identical corridors that were made of the black volcanic rock and had doors of spider-webs spun by black widows the size of small dogs.

"Tripper, I'm not sure about this," said Geneva.

"Don't turn chicken on me now."

"I'm not scared," said Geneva with clear offense. "But I think we're lost."

"Reckon I know where we is. Just follow me," said Tripper, pointing down the fifth corridor they had checked in the asylum. The spiders guarded the doors, but none moved to attack them.

"I'll take your word for it, but I think the corridors change as we walk."

"Yeah, but I can sense her aura." Pointing with his cane at a 'Y' shaped intersection, he said, "We roll down here."

"Whatever." She frowned. Her hair kept sticking up as if she were getting static shock.

Tripper glanced at her. "If'n there was ever anyone who looked like a witch, it's you right now."

Geneva laughed. "Careful, Mr. O'Sullivan, or I'll turn you into a toad!"

Tripper rolled his eyes and led her down the corridor, which ended in an incongruous steel door, like the type seen on a bank vault. It was not organic or volcanic like the rest of the asylum's construction. It was true steel, or whatever passed for steel in Hell.

Guarding it was a tiny alien that was known to Ops as one of the race of Subject Seven. Each member of the race had two arms and sat not on legs but a rather complex tail structure that made them look vaguely like snakes with arms. They wore golden spacesuits that were like body armor, or so it appeared. They had crash landed in Canada in 2004, and a specimen was brought back by Jennifer Saunders and her partners, Sheila Warren and Brent Jasper.[2]

The alien held up a rifle and said, "(&*(&^^^."

Tripper looked back at Geneva, who was guarding their rear, and said, "Y'all know any alien-speak?"

"I know ten languages and sixteen dialects, but lizard alien is not one of them," said Geneva ruefully.

"Great." Tripper looked at the alien and held up his hand in a gesture of peace. Sounding like an Indian in an old Western, he said, "I come in peace."

The alien gave him a look, shrugged, then opened the door as he said, "*()&*(*??. *&!"

"Uh, sure. Tip is in the mail," said Tripper as he walked in.

Geneva hesitated, wary of a trap. The alien gestured, looking perplexed by her behavior. Geneva finally shrugged and entered.

Inside was a padded cell typical of any asylum, also structured like a real building and not the faux organic structure of the rest of the building. And in the center of the cell were six people. There were three men and three women, all nude and covered with infected boils. The seventh person was Krissy, but only her head was visible. She was buried in the dirt floor, her head sticking up like a wart.

Obviously, the six people had been urinating on her for some time, for the room was soaked and reeked of urine. As soon as she took a breath, Geneva made a ghastly face and covered her nose.

Tripper didn't notice the smell. As old as he was, he pretty much couldn't smell anything unless it was right under his nose. What he

---

[2] Way back in the second of the two prelude novels, "Jennifer Saunders – Wendigo!" (2004)

did notice was Krissy, soaked in urine, her eyes closed, drinking it all in. Despite her efforts to drink, the urine was pooled around her neck.

"Krissy."

She opened her eyes and looked at him in astonishment. Trying to speak, she instead merely gurgled, her mouth full of urine but also from utter shock.

Tripper moved forward angrily. Using his cane like a mace, he batted aside two of the men. Geneva channeled and blew two of the women into the wall. The other two people ran.

Once they were gone, the floor around Krissy seemed to melt like hot butter. Then it appeared to vomit like a cat and leave Krissy standing on top of the dirt floor.

"My . . . uh, holy cow," said Krissy, her shock almost causing her to call on her Lord, a major transgression in Hell that would have led to something similar to electric shock. "Is it *you*? Again?"

"Reckon so. I been me for a long time now," said Tripper with a smile.

Krissy fell to her knees and grabbed his legs. Then she began sobbing and babbling.

Tripper glanced at Geneva with a 'help me' look. Geneva just rolled her eyes and said, "I think she's glad to see you."

Krissy suddenly babbled, "Please, please, get me out, out, *outttttttttttt!*"

"That's the plan. This place has guards — lizard aliens and black widows the size of m'lawn mower. Will they try to stop us?"

Krissy just nodded. "They don't care if you come in. But *no one* gets out again."

Tripper looked at Geneva. "Up for some spider-squishing?"

Geneva popped her right fist into her left palm. "More than willing, Mr. O'Sullivan!"

Tripper opened the door . . . and the battle was on.

Chapter Four
Nicole Alone . . . As Usual

"Ladies and germs, I promise it will get better soon at Ralph's Magic Show!"

There was dead silence from the crowd, but Nicole figured that made sense because the theatre seemed to be filled with only mannequins. They were a faceless army of white . . . although at least they packed the house.

In the five minutes since Nicole had awakened, she had concluded that Hell wasn't quite what she had expected. This was more like a bad nightmare caused by pizza and beer before bed after crashing for finals.

She was held captive in a metal standing cage akin to a bird cage, the cage inexplicably specifically to be exactly her size. Just for good measure, her wrists were chained to the sides of the cage, but she had no room to move anyhow. She stared through the bars at the crowd, but they were hard to see, for she was under a spotlight on the stage. Although she was nude, fishnet stockings were painted on her legs, and inexplicably her nipples and privates were gone, as if she, too, were a mannequin like the crowd. The silver bars were warm from the lights.

The theater was something she had seen in films, what one might expect in, say 1860s London. It smelled of candle wax, gas, and mold. The floorboards creaked with every move the magician made. The mannequins stacked both the main house and upper decks. The front of the stage was lit by candles that burned with inexplicable brightness. The atmosphere was strange. While the crowd was silent, the floorboard was constantly creaking and in the background a remix version of *Batdance* by Prince kept playing over . . . and over . . . and over.

The stage magician was a bizarre person. His name was Ralph, and his wrinkly old form was nude other than a red and black cape and matching magician's hat. He looked like . . . well, he looked like Albert Einstein, except instead of two eyes he had a single eye in the middle of his forehead and mere caverns where the eyes would be on a human. Ralph had a squeaky voice and talked and acted like a henpecked wife.

He also wasn't much of a magician. So far, he had failed to make the rabbit appear in his hat and had caught his penis on fire. Now he appeared to be messing with a caged carrier pigeon, which for some reason was bright orange.

Nicole was uncomfortable in her cage, unable to move, but initially had been more concerned about being separated from the others. She remembered seeing a giant wave of blood . . . then nothing. Obviously, Charon's ferry had been ambushed and capsized. . . she needed to escape and find them.

But that had proved difficult. She had no channeling ability whatsoever, so she had merely stood a prisoner, watching and waiting.

"Ralph, if I may offer some advice, as one entertainer to another, your act needs some work," said Nicole sympathetically.

Ralph nodded sadly and hung down his head like a boy who had dropped his last penny down the sewer grate. "I never was good at this."

"Is that why you're here?" she asked.

He looked at her. His single eye darted back and forth   it had no eyelid, so it was always looking, always watching. "Sort of. I got killed on stage. They said it was an electrical fault. I had gotten into torture magic trying to become a real magician . . . not a wise move. I never was very bright."

"I'm sorry. If you let me out, I can probably help."

"Sorry. I'm not a fan of this, but orders are orders."

"That's an old tune, Ralph. I've heard it from many men without courage or conviction," said Nicole.

Ralph shrugged. "Hey, if I had courage or conviction, I wouldn't be here in the *first* place. Sorry, doll."

With that, he pulled a white sheet off a table that had been covered. Fixated on her situation with tunnel vision, Nicole hadn't noticed it to the side.

"Oh, man," she said with a gasp. There were a dozen sharp, gleaming pirate swords on the table.

"Just so we're clear, this isn't personal. I'm under orders to soften you up," said Ralph apologetically.

"Soften me up? Those things will *kill* me," she shouted as he picked one up and swung it around.

"Not in Hell. But . . . boy, they hurt."

Then he impaled her right chest cavity, and she howled as if she were a thousand wolves howling at the full moon. She heard clapping and cheers from the mannequins in the office.

Nothing stopped the pain. She couldn't pass out. She could only suffer.

She knew this would drive her insane.

Ralphs picked up a second sword.

She held her breath.

But before he could advance, a hyena came racing in with a yellow envelope between its teeth. It spit the envelope at Ralph, then sat like a dog and said, "Fed Ex special, Ralph."

Ralph frowned. He took the envelope, which melted like butter when he touched it. That left the letter inside exposed, and he quickly read it.

Then he shook his head and looked at Nicole. "You've been summoned, and that overrides my job."

"Summoned?"

He waved the paper, which was some type of animal skin with symbolic writing in blood and bile. "She's higher than my paygrade down her, so you're going to her. No one gets out of a court summons in Hell. It's worse than a grand jury summons."

He moved forward and waved his hand. Her cage vanished, but she was in a yoke of bone. She was now totally nude, but her wound was gone, and her genitals had returned. It was like she had stepped out of the shower.

"I don't get it."

Before he could elaborate, sixteen nude Amazon savages appeared, all armed with gold spears and smiling with gold teeth. They were huge, all at least six-six, all with skin as black as night. They surrounded her, and one of them wrapped a rope of human ligaments around a hook on the front of the yoke. He began to lead her out of the theatre.

"Where are we going? Who are you taking me to?"

They stuck a spear in her left buttock.

"Owww! You guys have never heard of the "Me, too" movement, have you?"

They said nothing as they walked across a river of liquified fat using a bridge of hamster skeletons.

Held in the yoke of bone, Nicole was unable to resist, but she didn't see any point in trying. If someone wanted her, she wanted to know why they wanted her. Anything was better than being impaled by pirate swords.

She was marched on the points of spears by the savages to a large cave in the middle of a Hell forest that had living bodies instead of trees and dirt made of faces instead of, well, dirt. She bled from the pokes from the spears, but she avoided crying out in pain, understanding that Hell was purely a mental entity, so she wasn't suffering any real physical damage. Resistance was not only important, it was essential to survive Hell.

Surprisingly, the deeper they went, the more the jungle seemed real . . . authentic, that is, not a replication of a jungle based on vile, grotesque distortions. The dirt was dirt, the large trees were trees, the birds were birds . . . almost. They had an extra eye in the middle of their heads for some reason.

As they approached the cave, it looked like a giant, black mouth with overgrown moss serving as teeth. The jungle men prodded her to the entrance with the spears.

Once inside, she found herself on a red carpet leading to a throne that was made of gold. The floor was entirely sandstone set in cement. The walls were the same. The ceiling was shaped like the inside of a skull, and the only lighting was from two large men who were perpetually on fire on either side of the throne.

"Uh, you summoned me?" asked Nicole, surprised that the Amazons quickly released her and ran outside.

"I have," said the woman on the throne. The room was very dark, but suddenly there was an increase in the light as the woman said, "On your knees."

Nicole knelt, not an easy chore bound by the yoke, and noticed the room was oddly filled with background music — *I'm Your Boogeyman* by KC and the Sunshine Band.

"Really, I know this is Hell, but playing disco music is just going over the top," Nicole said nervously.

"Stop babbling."

Nicole gasped as the woman on the throne was suddenly visible in the light.

It was . . . *Nicole*.

Well, not *quite* Nicole. This woman was thinner, almost gaunt, and her eyes had dark circles offset by very pale skin. Nicole thought it was as if she had starved for two weeks and barely slept. Her right eye appeared blind, scar tissue around it. The woman was nude, but from the waist down she was painted black, as if someone had painted pants and boots on her. Her torso was nude with erect nipples. A wriggling earthworm hung from her belly button, which was really disturbing to Nicole.

"Who . . . are you?" asked Nicole from her knees.

"I am your future self . . . just call me Colie."

"Oh . . . okay. *Future* self?" asked Nicole, puzzled.

Colie glanced at the guards and shooed them away with a dismissive wave of her hand. Then she looked at Nicole. "Don't do anything foolish. You have no power here."

"I merely ask for information," said Nicole. "And I would like to stand."

"You will remain there." Colie sat on the throne and crossed her legs. "We'll have a girl-chat." There was nothing convivial about her tone.

"I'm not sure conversing with myself qualifies as a girl-chat, but we can try," said Nicole with a polite smile, as if she were a prospective employee and Colie her potential boss.

"You seem puzzled that I am a future self."

Nicole furrowed her brow. "That was not the impression I got of Hell from Geneva's explanations. Time seemed normal here — different from Earth time, but linear."

"For the most part, it is," said Colie, arching an eyebrow. The music in the background shifted to the soundtrack for the Netflix series *Jessica Jones*. "You see, it takes some real special pull to have a future-self and a past-self interact, but it *can* happen. I felt it important to talk to you."

"So you say. But this is likely all lies, for after all, this is Hell."

"Do you truly believe this is all a lie?" asked Colie with a sly smile.

Nicole paused, and after a moment said, "No . . . no, I do not. I'm not sure *what* this is about, but I somehow . . . *know* you."

"And I know you. Obviously. And much better than you know yourself. I'm going to show you what's going to land you here, unless you make dramatic changes."

Nicole smirked. "That should be funny."

"*Shut the fuck up, you arrogant little bitch!*" shouted Colie, and her words echoed as did the slap she applied to Nicole's right cheek. "You always fucking think you know everything and think you are fucking right! You engage in horrible acts and think they don't affect you. They do! *You turn into the monsters you tried to stop!*"

Stunned, Nicole said, "This is a lie, a trick. I am not some dead soul already psychologically primed to be here, you gaunt slut. I am Nicole Smith, and I am *alive*."

"That . . . that oversight can be corrected. Guards!"

The sixteen savage jungle dwellers returned. They pulled Nicole to her feet. Colie put one hand on her hip and with another she pointed to the door. "Take her to the Land of a Thousand Pains. I'll be there shortly to begin breaking her soul into its component parts. Move!"

Nicole cursed as she was dragged away.

One of the guards remained behind. Colie snapped at him, "What do *you* want?"

Despite being an Amazon jungle warrior, the woman spoke with a clipped French accent. "If you are her, you know what will happen here with this invasion . . . she's going to escape, obviously, right?"

Colie smirked. "Don't think too much, imbecile. You'll hurt your head. Get to work!"

She left. Then Colie moved behind a curtain of whale skin to a large, body-size mirror held in a frame of black pearls. Waving, she activated a communicator, and an image became clear in the mirror.

"I've done as you asked," she told the man on the other side.

"Good," said a voice that sounded like a female computer opening an elevator.

"I'm not sure what it's going to accomplish. She got arrogant, so I sent her to the Land of a Thousand Pains. I know that wasn't the plan."

"Don't worry about it. You're angry at her."

"Angry at myself . . . I was very arrogant when alive. I was forced into a bad situation, of course, but I was arrogant. It was my downfall."

"It's good you see that in yourself."

"A bit late now," she said, smiling to her new friend, obscured by the poor transmission through the mirror.

"Well, don't worry about it. As long as you've accomplished this, there's no point in staying. Make your way to her and destroy the memory lock. Our long-term objectives begin there."

"What are you doing while I'm doing that?"

"Talking to another set of old friends. See you."

Then she was gone.

Colie bit her lip and then glared at the mirror. Then she punched it, smashing it into a thousand fragments, sickened by her true reflection.

Whispering to her jagged image, she said, "How did I ever wind up this way? How did I get so bad?"

Then she turned and exited, gesturing and winding up in the Land of a Thousand Pains.

The land was well named. Nicole screamed as she was pulled on a stretching rack made of bone. She felt her ligament and tendons pop. The pain was agonizing.

"Knock It off," said Colie to the four purple, horned aliens operating the rack. "Go take a piss break or something."

Nicole groaned. She knew the pain wasn't physical, that it was all mental, but she couldn't make it stop hurting.

Colie leaned over the rack and glared at Nicole. "Arrogant bitch. You're hiding because *you don't remember.*"

"Give up the games, woman. I have work to do here," Nicole snapped, sounding braver than she felt. Her face was contorted with pain.

"No, you must remember what you've done. It's your only hope for redemption. Your subconscious is trying to protect you, but it's doing more harm than good."

Colie put her right hand on Nicole's forehead.

Suddenly, Nicole was in the past.

Chapter Five
Sylvester and Old Enemies

"It's been many a moon since I was hit that hard," muttered Sylvester as he awakened slowly and rolled over onto his side. He rubbed his head. He was nude other than a cheetah-print loincloth worth of Tarzan.

Slowly, he realized he was in some type of backyard. The sod was fresh and well groomed, there was a small pool, and a solid wooden fence kept away the rest of the neighbors. Typical middle-class America . . . except that past the fence the sky was red, and Sylvester could hear volcanos erupting and the screams of those in torment. Oh, and on closer examination, he realized the grass blades were really painted fingers.

Then he remembered the ambush of the ferry . . . where were the others?

"Rough trip?"

Recognizing the voice, he turned and was surprised to see the voice he recognized did *not* match the figure before him. The voice was that of the late Trixie Taylor, the torture magician who was also a doctor. However, before him stood a nude and frankly ugly, gangly girl with no breasts or hips, despite being fourteen years old. She had dull hair, a dull face, and blazing red eyes. Leaning against a horse carriage pulled by a horse made of flame, she smiled and put a hand on her hip. "I guess it was. You haven't said shit yet."

"Trixie?" he asked to confirm, getting slowly to his feet. He immediately focused and modified his clothing. He now was fully clothed in a black and white pinstriped suit with an odd, green archer's hat.

"Yes. Welcome to my little corner of Hell."

"You look different," he said. Taylor had been incinerated a few months earlier on Mars by the Four Cornered Wheel in combat, according to the report Sylvester had read from Jennifer Saunders.[3]

"I used a glamour," and she pointed up, to indicate Earth, "up there."

"I knew that. I could see through the glamour. Even at that, you look different . . . a child."

Sinisterly, she licked her lips, and he could see her teeth were stained with blood. "Child? There are no children in Hell. Let's just say I'm . . . younger."

"And more innocent?"

"I was *never* innocent," she said with a laugh. "I killed my first victim when I was thirteen, and believe me, I was fully aware of what I was doing." She looked around and shrugged like a bored game show host. "All in all, I pretty much cemented my trip here before I got out of high school."

"Something you seem proud of."

Her face darkened and she shook her head. "No. Not anymore . . . but, trust me, no one puts themselves here *alone*. Society helps you out a lot."

Sylvester chuckled and said, "Aye, that's an old tune, Doctor Taylor, and old excuse."

She smiled wickedly. "I think it is, too. Anyhow, if being a kid bugs you, would you prefer my glamorous, glamour self?"

"Ah. 'Tis irrelevant to me. It is your choice."

She morphed and changed into the image she always projected when alive — a tall woman with wavy red hair, with a large chest, perfect legs and bottom, and bright blue eyes. Her face was a plastic

---

[3] In TM 3.11 "Red Kelkirkstadt"

surgeon's dream. Her smile was wide, her teeth bright, and her eyes a deep blue. When using her glamour, she also changed her outfit mentally, and now she wore a doctor's white slacks, a blue shirt, a white jacket, and a stethoscope. "Am I suitably dressed as a stereotypical HMO primary care rep?"

He studied her. "Why am I here? Who capsized the ferry?"

Coyly, she smiled and said, "Oh, so many questions."

"And few answers," said Sylvester, starting to look around for a trap.

"Oh, those are coming," said a male voice to Sylvester's right.

Startled, the Immortal Man turned and saw former International News Network (INN) founder, CEO, and President — and long-time torture magician — Gary Hart.

Hart was a stunningly handsome man with a firm jaw, black straight hair parted to the right, blue eyes, and a way of smiling that made it look like he was looking right into your thoughts. Always dressed impeccably and expensively, even in Hell, he was wearing a blue suit vest, white shirt, blue slacks, and an expensive Rolex. He had a martini in his right hand. Despite being in the middle of Hell, he looked exactly as he might have after a board meeting at the INN offices.

Born to the son of a Hollywood couple in 1938, Hart was kidnapped by a TM when he was twelve. That led him to twenty years of TM activity. He was good at it, and quickly rose through the ranks. But he was much better at controlling events *behind* the scenes. As he discovered, that was where real power existed. In 1975, he gave up his TM career to found INN, convinced cable TV would be a reality within ten years. He was right.

However, he still worshipped Quafara and Elkrod, the first torture magicians. He greatly aided their manifestation in 2012. And after Ops sent them back to Hell, he attempted to resurrect them. That attempt in January 2018 led to his death and hence his presence in Hell.

Sylvester chuckled. "Well, I would say this is a surprise, but quite honestly, it obviously is not."

Hart held up the drink and took a sip. "I would tend to agree with you, Sylvester. Good to see you survived the ferry attack."

"Survived?"

"Well, you know what I mean. Everything is relative here. But you *can* get your soul permanently destroyed in Hell," said Hart, making a polite face but also delivering a clear warning. "Rare, but it happens."

"Point taken. To what do I owe the honor of the attention of two such gracious hosts?"

Trixie deferred to Hart. Hart said cautiously, "Your arrival here has been noticed and is going to upset the politics. It's a chance for Trixie and I to save Hell from domination under Hitler."

Sylvester frowned, then nodded once. "Surely you are aware why myself and the others are here?"

"Yes, to stop the Horal." Hart smiled, but his eyes were cold. And Trixie, to his side, just looked worried. Hart added, "Which we all know is impossible."

"Do we?" asked Sylvester with a sly smile.

"You do. I do. Trixie does. Does anyone else matter?"

Sylvester shook his head. "No. And you are correct."

"So that isn't why you're *really* here."

"I have reasons," said Sylvester with a sly half-smile.

Hart chuckled. "Playing the manipulator is not your game, Immortal Man. You spent too many decades hiding from humanity and pretending you weren't part of it to truly understand the complexity of human nature. If you're not here for the Horal, then I can think of only one other reason you are here."

Sylvester stared at him for several seconds. "So be it. Will you attempt to stop me?"

Hart laughed, er, heartily. "Stop you? Far from it, old man. You might succeed, which would benefit us all. But meanwhile, we have to deal with Hitler. Certainly, he is the biggest obstacle to any of your objectives, stated or unstated."

"Aye, I would concur, knowing of Hitler."

"He's much more powerful here, and he's made his move. He's already taken control of the ninth circle, but he hasn't yet been able to expand to the other circles. But he's close, so we had been preparing to make a move. Are you in?"

"Of course," said Sylvester, and they shook hands.

"I've gathered some allies," said Trixie. She shook her head and said, "Damn, Sylvester, you wouldn't believe how hard it is to get someone to go up against Hitler down here. It's like looking for a volunteer for medical experiments in Siberia."

Sylvester gave a wry smile. "Your charm didn't help?"

Rolling her eyes, she crooked her finger and led him across the lawn, their footsteps breaking fingers as they advanced, Hart following behind them, as she said, "My charm extends to performing surgery without anesthesia for an exorbitant fee. Anyhow, I *did* find three allies who will align all the way with us."

Now that they were closer, the pool area metamorphosized into one that looked like a five-star hotel, with an Olympic sized pool that was *true* water, a rarity in Hell. There were many white pool tables and chairs, white curtains, and a pleasantly painted orange deck.

Sitting by the pool were two people, lounging on chairs made of human bone and cartilage. One was a tall, gorgeous blond with long, straight hair that was braided into a tail in back. She had round, blue eyes, supple red lips, and lanky legs. Her features were perfect. Wearing a yellow tunic and matching pleated skirt and boots, she looked horribly misplaced in the landscape of hell.

The other person was a tall, handsome man with curly dark hair, dark eyes, and a smoldering smile. He wore white body armor with light blue trim, looking like a cross between a medieval and futuristic warrior.

"Meet Gwen and Lancelot."

Sylvester looked at her with surprise. "*The* Gwen and Lancelot?"

"Yup."

Sylvester looked at Hart. "I thought they were fictional."

Hart shrugged and sipped his drink, then said, "So did we."

Gwen rose and approached Sylvester, flanked by Lancelot on her right. She extended her hand. "Mr. Hart has explained who you are and why you are here. Our loyalty is yours."

"I . . . appreciate that. I just . . . pardon me, but knowing you are real and in Hell is what the youngsters would call a double whammy."

Lance said, "We cheated on the greatest King in the history of the world and our lust destroyed Camelot. Where else would we go?"

Sylvester nodded sadly, accepting the argument.

"I'm a little offended you think we're not real. We know Chaucer's works survived," said Gwen.

"They did. It . . . that is unimportant now." Sylvester turned to Trixie. "You said you found *three* allies."

"I did," said Trixie with the same dark, cold smile she previously used on those she was about to medically experiment on as torture. "Here comes the third. I'm sure you know her."

"Hi, Sylvester. We meet again."

Sylvester snapped around and was horrified to see before him a sixteen-year-old girl with wavy black hair cut short, black eyes, and a very round face with round lips that gave her the look of a bird. She had a pleasing physical form and was completely nude.

"Terri Sparrow," said Sylvester, his voice a whisper. "You can't be here."

"Oh, I can," she said, keeping her distance from the group, staying near the lawn. "Being your first torture victim and spending weeks as your rape toy didn't absolve me for my sins *before* that. The three years as a prostitute and thief sent me here. I never had a chance at redemption. Traumatized, I killed myself a day after you released me, convinced you would return to finish your devilish work."

Sylvester turned to Hart and snapped, "I will not work with this woman."

"You will, or you will never get off this property. We'll turn your soul into chewing gum and spit you into the ninth level," said Hart coldly, dumping his drink into the pool, causing it to bubble.

Sparrow spoke gently. "Your guilt too much for you, Sylvester?"

He snarled and said, "Very well. Our mutual needs are far more important than . . . discomfort."

Trixie laughed. "Hey, it's comfortable for *us* watching you squirm like a fish on a hook."

Sparrow said, "Oh, Sylvester, we all have need of you. And you have need of us." She paused. "Never forget that."

"She speaks the truth, sir," said Lance.

Sylvester and Sparrow stared at each other. It was impossible for Sylvester to avoid thinking of how he had kidnapped and held her prisoner for weeks, raping her daily, torturing her with burns, whippings, anything he could think of. He was an angry, bitter teen seeking power in a world that had spit on him. Having control over her had been exhilarating.

He felt that surge of anger and lust now.

He fought it back.

Barely.

Turning to Hart, who was smiling with amusement because he was quite aware of Sylvester's internal struggle, Sylvester said, "What is the plan?"

"Complicated. Sit down and we'll explain while we track down one of your partners in particular, one we must have. Explanations will take a while, because, like LA traffic, this place is quite a mess."

Chapter Six
Evil Saving Good?

"This is one messy job!" shouted Geneva as she channeled wind to send two by fours made of bone and other objects at the myriad of dog-sized, female black widow spiders charging them from the three corridors — one ahead, one to the right, and one to the left. Krissy stood behind her. Spider guts covered all three of them.

"No foolin', Kane!" shouted Tripper, using his cane to help direct his channeling. He was simply rupturing earth and flipping the spiders into each other. Then they started devouring each other.

A bigger problem was the myriad of two-foot-tall Subject Seven aliens. They were like ants at a picnic.

"Trip, we gotta get outta here!" shouted Geneva, not in panic, but simply to be heard over the din of battle.

"I'm with y'all there, reckon! Hold tight."

Tripper suddenly aimed upwards and channeled earth and wind simultaneously, rupturing the asylum. Then he channeled a furious wind to lift them out of the corridor.

"Yiiiiiiiiiiii!" shouted Krissy as the three of them were lifted into the air to the roof.

But the spiders fought back, shooting webs out their asses. One caught Krissy. Tripper had hold of her and didn't let go, so something had to give. It was Krissy. Her right leg suddenly ripped off.

"Aghhhhhhhhh! I hate when this happens!" she shouted as the trio landed hard on the roof, Krissy's blood flying everywhere.

"Your leg!" shouted Geneva.

Krissy waved her off. "This is Hell. This shit happens all the time. Hold on." She strained like a constipated woman on the toilet, and within seconds, her body was hole again. Better yet, she was no longer nude, now wearing a light blue camisole and jeans shorts with black boots, for foot protection and not just style.

"Let's get the fuck outta here," she said.

The spiders were now ascending the walls and had them surrounded. The roof itself was flat and slippery as glass.

"Sticky feet or not, they aren't standing up here," said Geneva, and she channeled wind furiously to blow them away.

"Reckon this ain't gonna work forever!" shouted Tripper.

Geneva looked over the edge and saw spiders filling the streets like floodwaters. They were starting to climb the crystal wall that marked the edge of the city to prepare to leap on them, as the building was separated from the wall only by a few feet due to an alley at ground level.

"I really hate this place," said Krissy.

"There we agree," said Geneva. "Trip! Take over blowing them back for a bit. I've got an idea."

"Go for it."

Seamlessly, Tripper assumed wind control. Geneva turned to the gigantic crystal wall. She focused on it. Concentrating with everything she had, mixing in probability cloud influx and trying to draw on the changes in her channeling after being hit by a tachyon surge by Calico Kelkirk, she sent forth a bizarre channel. And she felt a crack in the seam and exploited that.

The most ear-shattering crack ever shot through the valley, and instantly everyone froze, as if the earth itself had split into half.

Then the crystal began to flow at them as if in a wave.

"Hold tight!" shouted Geneva, taking Tripper with her right hand and Krissy with her left. Then she focused and, like a surfer, rode out the crystal wave, which flew them over buildings and across several square miles. They flew out of the city and soared along as if in a flash flood, carried to a crash landing . . . somewhere.

"Uhhhhhhhhhhhhhhhh," said Geneva, pushing herself to her feet. She got to her knees and looked around. Krissy was next to her, also getting up. Tripper was a few yards away, laying on his back, reaching for his cane with his right hand.

"That was some ride," said Krissy, hitting her head and shaking her ears like a swimmer with water in the ear, but in her case, she was shaking out spider guts.

Geneva moved and stood over Tripper. "Had enough yet, old man?"

"Whippersnapper, reckon this is just the warm-up. But help an old man up."

She helped him up and retrieved his cane. They looked around. They were on something that looked like the Utah salt flats, but they were next to a race track. Bizarrely, it was like a child's electronic car track, only life-size. Embedded in the tracks were live human heads, all wailing and screaming, in lanes one through six. Lane seven, the inside lane, was free of obstruction. The trio was standing on the outside lanes. Further down the track were spectators. Inside the oval of the track were about a hundred men and women being crucified. They all moaned, bled, and struggled futility to escape.

"Not really NASACAR approved," muttered Tripper.

"It's horrible, but don't dwell on it," warned Geneva.

He nodded. Then he saw a red booth made of some type of animal skin and sitting in it was a man Tripper knew. The man was blond, tall at six feet and four inches, and had a huge nose. His blue eyes were dark and his frame withered, as if he were anorexic. He was nude but without genitals. He held a starter's pistol in his right hand, and he rose.

"Now I know why we landed here," said Tripper.

Before Geneva could ask for clarification, the man fired the pistol, and the six cars took off. Heads popped like tomatoes and bled everywhere as the cars raced through to the screams of the assembled crowd, mostly human but with a few alien races mixed in, along with one very bored looking cow.

Tripper walked across the salt flats to the booth, which was like a lifeguard tower and elevated about three feet in the air on human bone. The man looked down and laughed hysterically.

"Nice to know he has a sense of humor," said Krissy nervously.

"Care to introduce yourself?" shouted Geneva to him.

"I'm sorry, pretty ones. Tripper! You dog! What year is it now?"

"2021."

"Nein! By der further, it's been 75 years! You just got your skinny ass down here?"

"Yup, reckon so."

The man jumped down and shook Tripper's hand furiously. "You look the same."

"Y'all is just sayin' that to flatter me. I'm a lot older and uglier."

"Yet you get the frauleins," said the man, winking.

"A-hem!" said Geneva.

"Oh, sorry. This here is Dirk Haughter. He was a double-agent in the Nazi camp who helped us penetrate Hitler's compound the day we finished the fucker off. How did you get here?"

"Ah, well, I still found time to enjoy the power of the Nazis . . . and had some issues post-war. A little rape and murder . . . nothing that big." He shrugged. "And once I was here and found the races, well, you get used to the smell."

Geneva made a face. Krissy ignored them and said to Tripper. "So why did we land next to *him*?"

Tripper looked at Dirk. "We're goin' after the big guy again. He's trying to take over, and we came from Earth to stop his ass."

Dirk raised an eyebrow. "So, you're alive."

"Yup."

"Interesting. My, my. *Quite* the day."

"Y'all in or out, kraut?"

Haughter laughed. "I'm in, of course. What could be more exciting?"

"You need more help than him," said a female voice behind them.

Tripper and Geneva turned and were stunned to see two females they knew.

Geneva snorted. "Well, it's not a shock seeing you two here."

The two women, who looked to be in their twenties, turned and looked at each other with coy, sexy looks. They were each wearing pink bikinis and sunglasses, and each were covered in blood splatter.

"Don't be a pill, Kane," said the woman on the right.

"Yeah. We're here to help," said the woman on the left.

The women were Lisa and Sherry McGrath — Little Jack's sister and stepsister.

Lisa was a thin but well-built, sexy brunette with long, chestnut brown hair that extended halfway down her back. It was straight. She had a round face, supple lips, green eyes, and freckles. Clearly, she worked out to stay in shape and liked to be tan.

Sherry was a bit more buxom, also with chestnut brown hair, but hers was wavy and framed a more sexual face. She did not have freckles, but she also had green eyes.

Tripper said with a glare, pointing his cane at Sherry, "I done had enough of y'all's help back when y'all ambushed me in Tupelo."

In October of 2017, Sherry had posted as a client and visited Tripper at his Tricky Dick Detective Agency in Tupelo. She claimed her sister had gone missing in Fulton, a small town about twenty miles to the east. That was a set up allowing Little Jack to ambush and come within a hair's breadth of killing Tripper.[4]

Sherry smiled. "Aw, c'mon, that was a long time ago."

Lisa saw the look on Geneva and Tripper's face and quickly added, "We really *are* here to help. Little Jack's . . . conversion . . . on Earth, it has, we've been told, given us a chance to redeem our souls."

Sherry added, "Yeah, when we got here, we were . . . not popular. We were held in this land where the animals reign and we were eaten alive by jackals endlessly, while chained to a tree of bone. It   we were evil, incestuous bitches. But we've learned, and Little Jack has given us a chance to save our souls by saving his own."

---

[4] See TM 2.8 "Family Matters"

Geneva gave Tripper a highly skeptical look, but she knew it wasn't her choice. "It's your call, Trip. After all, it is you they tried to kill."

He shrugged, took off his cap, then put it back on before saying, "Y'all forgot, they also stiffed me on the bill. But I can get over it. So . . . ladies . . . what can you offer?"

"Transportation. Believe me, people know you're here, and they'll do a lot to stop you and drag you to Hell forever, hold you here for endless revenge," said Lisa. "Mize. Elkrod. Quafara. Jill Tifton. Hell, I've heard even Nixon has a grudge with you, Tripper."

"He's just mad I didn't vote for him in '72. Fine."

Lisa pointed at one of the race cars. "We own the flats. We can use one of these cars and get into the fiefdom where Hitler reigns. It will keep us safe from attack."

Geneva folded her arms over her chest and jutted out a sexy hip. "What do you get out of this?"

Surprisingly, Krissy spoke. "It's a Hell thing. They've been given a shot at redemption by Little Jack's actions. Believe me, changing your character and praying a lot works. But God won't get them out unless they *prove* they've taken their brother's works to heart."

Lisa nodded and said, "Basically, that's it."

Tripper looked at Krissy incredulously. "Y'all mean after torturing and killing people, not to mention all the robbery and incest and stiffin' me on my bill, God will let them outta here?"

"Yep."

Tripper threw his hat in the air, caught it, and put it back on. "That's a ball of shit for sure."

"It's God's mercy," said Geneva. "I will accept it for now. I've told Sam Grant, I do not accept this place, but I can't do anything about that for now. You two get us to Hitler's fiefdom and your duty to us is ended."

Lisa and Sherry clapped eagerly like girls inducted into a sorority.

Dirk looked at Hitler. "I told you, you get all the sexy frauleins."

Chapter Seven
Kress' Visions

"Uhhhhhhh," moaned Kress, slowly opening her eyes, despite her desire to keep them shut. She knew something had happened in the attack, had felt the pull of a portal. She could be anywhere, though she knew she was still in Hell.

Slowly, she opened her eyes, just the right one first. Cautiously, she tested her muscles. She didn't appear to be bound, and she seemed to be lying on her back.

Her eyes slowly saw light, then a picture appeared. Blue sky. There were towering buildings around her . . . where was she?"

Slowly, she rolled to her right and got to her knees. Then she gasped.

She knew precisely where she was. Oslo. Her company, Pentagon Fifth Financial, owned the large, brown, 80-story high rise that she was kneeling before on the sidewalk.

"I'm . . . back?"

Maybe she had portaled out of Hell to escape the capsizing ferry? This was weird.

She was near the door, which was glass. The only odd thing was the utter lack of activity. It was sunlight and daytime, so there should have been plenty of people around. But the streets and sidewalks were empty, creating an eerie silence that was somehow more intimidating than a cadre of B-2 bombers would have been.

Kress suddenly realized she was dressed, wearing a turquoise turtleneck, jeans, and white boots. The look fit her, but these weren't her clothes . . . were they?

Confused, she approached the door. There was no security, and the door opened before she touched it.

Now she was suspicious. She moved to the lobby and punched in the button floor the eightieth floor, the first of her two-floor penthouse home and office. After Calico Kelkirk came to power and shifted political and economic capital in the organization, Kress travelled a lot and spent probably no more than a few weeks a year in the penthouse. But it was still hers.

The elevator ascended. It stopped. The door slowly opened.

She prepared for anything, except what she actually got.

The penthouse seemed normal. The elevator opened into a marble bay with plastic plants that led to a reception area. It was normal, but vacant. Passing through the door, she found her way to her office.

The office was decorated in perfectly normal business European with tasteful landscapes, neutral colors, and a large desk.

The only oddity was the chair behind the desk was turned around, back facing her, so she couldn't see who was sitting in it.

Then it spun.

She screamed in horror as she realized who the figure was in the chair.

A Horal.

"Stop it! Get with it!" shouted a woman, slapping Kress hard.

Kress shook her head, realizing things had changed. Before her was a woman she didn't know, but behind her were several people, and she did know one of them. "Sylvester!"

He smiled and moved forward.

She now realized she was held in a cage of the bone of a woolly mammoth. The mammoth however, had a normal head and was still 'alive,' whatever that meant in Hell. "Nice having ya, kid."

"Huh?" said Kress, helped through a gate in the skeleton by Gwen and Lancelot. They somehow dematerialized her, and she simply stepped through and regained her form on the outside.

Kress took in the place. They were on a plain of lava rock, volcanoes everywhere. The sky was red. She was now nude, her hundreds of portal tattoos obvious.

Sylvester said, "You can create clothes. My new friends helped me find you. We still have to find the others."

"I . . . I . . . there was a . . . Horal." She shook her head and focused on clothes, dressing herself in some sort of metal, skin-like outfit she had seen in a sci-fi film once. From the neck down, she looked like a metal mannequin.

"A nightmare. The mammoth is a beast of nightmares in Hell," said Trixie.

"Aw, you'll make me blush with compliments," said the mammoth.

Kress frowned, studying Sylvester's team. "I know you. Tricia Taylor?"

"Trixie. Nice to meet you," said Trixie, wearing a doctor's scrubs. She held out a blood-soaked hand and said, "The blood is dry. It represents the blood on my hands."

Kress didn't shake Taylor's hands, instead pointing at Hart. "I know you, too."

"I'm Gary Hart. Charmed."

"I know what you really did and who you were, Hart. I'm not so charmed, but I guess we're in this together," said Kress. She didn't shake his hand. "Who are these two?"

"Lady Gwen and Lancelot," said Sylvester, clearly lost in thought.

"From *King Arthur*?" asked Kress incredulously. "You're real?"

"Indeed, we are," said Lancelot. They exchanged greetings.

Kress then asked Sylvester. "Who put me here?"

"I don't know. We found you. We need you to execute the plan, of course," he said grimly. Then he quickly said, "Uh, our final partner, this woman is my first torture victim, Terri Sparrow."

"Uhhhhhhhhhhhh . . . hi," said Kress nervously.

"Good day," said Terri without a smile but with a firm handshake. Then Kress asked Sylvester. "The ferry capsized. We were attacked, right? That's what I remember."

"Yes. We were separated. Hart pulled me towards his area — things are far more complex than we thought."

"Who attacked us?" asked Kress.

"It's being investigated. Come, let us ride while I catch you up."

A taxi arrived. Of course, a taxi in Hell wasn't quite the Yellow Cab of a New York street. This taxi was a giant slug that had a cab of skeleton and a cover of human skin. Stairs were embedded into the slug's side. The team ascended and took seats. Sylvester was at the head, and to his right were Hart and Trixie, to his left Kress and Sparrow. Gwen and Lance were across and standing, serving as guards.

"I feel a little rocky," said Kress, rubbing her mouth with her sleeve.

"Hell does that at first," said Hart, sipping his seemingly bottomless drink.

Kress shook her head. "It's not Hell. I can handle *Hell* — I mean, I'm not stuck here. I can brand myself and get out whenever I want. It's the *Horal*."

"You say you saw one, but that was undoubtedly delusion," said Sylvester, waving her off.

But Kress shook her head. "No. It was some type of warning. Believe me, I know the difference."

Hart and Trixie glanced at each other and looked skeptical. Sylvester looked at them and said, "You must forgive our . . . ally. Her skills got us here, but she has her own issues with the Horal."

"I'm telling you, it was a warning! *Shut up and listen to me!*" she shouted.

Gwen stepped forward. "Be calm, woman."

"Kress, we established the Horal can't exist here. Hell is the creation of the psyche of man; hence, no Horal," said Sylvester, rehashing the argument they'd had in New Mexico at the Plain of Sorrows when all this started.

"You're wrong. Our theory is bullshit. The Horal are everywhere. But, fine, fine. Don't believe me," snapped Kress. "Fine. When this all turns into a shitstorm and you get your dick cut off, don't come crying to me."

Sylvester studied her. "What would it be a warning about?"

"I . . . don't know. Maybe it's just letting us know that they know we're here."

"Perhaps," said Sylvester. "But it doesn't matter, Carole. Whether the Horal know we're here or not, they certainly will by the time we find them."

Sullenly, Kress said, "Yeah, I guess so."

Hart smiled. "Sylvester, you clearly have your plans set."

Sylvester nodded. "Our plan works regardless of what Carole saw. If the Horal are not here, or if they are but scattered throughout Hell, we must congregate at the source of power. Aye, we must go to the ninth circle."

"Uh, for those of us that haven't read Dante, what's there?" asked Kress.

Gwen shook her head. "That is the seat of power. Dante's Hell is divided into nine circles, the ninth circle being divided further into four rings, their boundaries only marked by the depth of their sinners' immersion in the ice. Satan sits in the last ring. Even Dante kept his mouth shut when he visited and hasn't gone back there since. The worst sinners are in the fourth ring of the ninth circle, the betrayers to their benefactors. When Dante was here, they were frozen into the ice, completely unable to move or speak as they be contorted into all sorts of grotesque shapes as a part of their punishment."

Lance interjected, "Hell stays modern, though. Nowadays the punishments are different, but the rankings are the same."

Kress made a face. "It sounds very organized."

Sylvester said, "So is the human mind."

Hart studied Sylvester. "Let's discuss this a minute." He sipped his drink. Sylvester noticed his face breaking out in pimples and he was being buzzed by flies. That told Sylvester Hart was starting to stress and break down his psychic ability to maintain proper human form.

"Very well," said Sylvester.

"Let's talk about the Big Man for a bit. Satan was formerly the Angel of Light before he tried to usurp the power of God. As punishment, God banished his lame ass out of Heaven to an eternity in Hell as the ultimate sinner." Hart sipped his drink, then continued. "But he hasn't always been the Big Guy here. Dante met him. Satan received the same punishments in Hell as the rest of the sinners."

Trixie shook her head. "Uh, Gary, I've seen pictures of him from some of the runners here. He's a giant demon, frozen to the torso in ice at the center of Hell. He has three faces and a pair of bat-like wings under each chin that beat and keep the Ninth Circle frozen. In his three mouths, he chews on Judas Iscariot, Marcus Junius Brutus, and Gaius Cassius Longinus."

"Who are those guys?" asked Kress.

Obviously irritated, Gwen said, "Judas betrayed Jesus, Brutus was the key assassin of Cesar, and Longinus was the instigator of the plot to assassinate Cesar. Know you nothing of history?"

"Hey, religion is for idiots. And I have other things to remember," said Kress defensively.

Gwen turned to Sylvester. "Must we suffer this child?"

"I'm afraid so. She's vital." He turned back to Hart. "What fact do you seek to elucidate, Hart? That Satan is not truly in charge of the ninth circle?"

Hart just smiled with a shit-eating grin.

Sylvester laughed. "Then who is in charge?"

"I don't know. It changes a lot."

Sylvester frowned. "This changes nothing. We must still get to the ninth circle to deal with the Horal."

Lancelot pulled his sword. "I shall take us there. But our road shall not be easy."

Sylvester nodded. "Nothing worth doing ever is."

Chapter Eight
Nicole's Crime

Not sure this was worth doing, but not entirely sure why she couldn't stop the memory either, Nicole lay on the stretching rack in the Land of a Thousand Pains and, forced by Colie, remembered her past.

But to her horror, she would realize it was a past she had forgotten . . . a repressed memory.

December 9, 2017. The desert outside Palm Springs.

Nicole arrived at the set for a shoot of yet another snuff film that warm, winter morning. She parked behind the faux prison set that Sunset and Morgana's team had assembled for the film.

Nicole was nervous. She knew she was at a critical point with her infiltration of the two torture magicians' website, knew that they were the ones that had ordered her father's agent, Helena, to kill him. Or, as Helena claims, they killed him themselves. It didn't matter. They were guilty

Angry, she sat in the car and remembered the day In 2015 when, as a freshman at USC, her mother on her deathbed had revealed her father's heart attack was poison, not a natural death. That led her to Helena, who was a TM and threw Nicole off the roof. Nicole manifested her channeling for the first time and survived. Helena and her acolyte turned up dead.

Nicole had wanted to go undercover in snuff films to hunt down the TMs involved, but her BFF and roommate, Audrey, talked her out of it. But in April, Audrey had died from a rare and terrible disease. Now alone, Nicole, a theatre actress just like her late father, went undercover in June as actress Stacy Carpenter.

She had made progress. Dark Death Fetish website was run by a mother-daughter team, Morgana and Sunset. Now forty, Morgana was tall with black hair like Nicole's, but it was laced with gray. Her skin was very good, so she either took really good care of it, used a lot of make-up, or was using a glamour. Knowing what Nicole knew, she suspected the latter. Morgana had tattoos, but they were well hidden. Her long, black hair hid them well, but Nicole was observant and caught, oddly, tattoos of numbers on Morgana's upper back and shoulders.

Sunset now handled the day-to-day routine of the business. Now twenty-six, Sunset was a very pretty woman with long, curvy and curly blonde hair that she wore past her shoulders. She had pretty blue eyes, a thin but attractive frame, freckles, and a winning smile.

They were TMs. That was obvious. Nicole made no secret, no attempt to hide her aura, and they were slowly introducing her to being a TM acolyte. Slowly.

Nicole wasn't worried about Morgana in a battle. But Sunset had paranormal power beyond just TM, based on Nicole's aural reads over the last six months. Now, Nicole was no plain ol' channeler either, but she had no idea what she was getting into with combating Sunset.

Sadly, Nicole didn't know that Morgana and Sunset had been aware of Nicole's deception from the very start.

Unusual for December, the day was very hot, very dry, very windy as a Santa Ana was moving in rapidly. Nicole hated the weather, caused by high pressure in the right spot pushing hot desert winds inland. The low humidity dried out her skin and made her lips and fingernails crack, even with moisturizer. And God help her hair.

Nicole wore a police officer's uniform, as befit the script. She exited and locked her car, bringing her white purse with her towards a card table where some doughnuts and coffee were set up. Although it was only nine in the morning, it was already 82 degrees due to the Santa Ana.

When Nicole exited, she saw, as usual, Morgana's black Mercedes parked near the main staging area for the set. The prison set was open, other than one small area that had a roof. As a result, sand was blowing on the set. They were in the middle of nowhere, as befit a script of drunk sorority girls getting captured while on vacation in Mexico.

Morgana wore a white blouse with matching pants and a black leather belt that crisscrossed. She was tan, dry, and irritable. "Hi, Stacy. C'mon, you can help us out."

Sunset appeared around the corner. She wore blue jeans and a dark purple, short-sleeved top that had sparking stars. She wore a crucifix necklace. "Hey, yeah. Let's blow the set clean."

Nicole put her purse down on the table and said, "It's going to blow right back. The winds are brutal."

"I know, but we can set up a wall over here," said Sunset, and using TK she moved some of the portable walls for one of the cells to block the bulk of the wind. It was effective.

"That works, but you've cut our sets in half," said Morgana to her daughter.

Sunset shrugged. "Deal with it, mom."

Morgana looked at Nicole. "Is that any way for a daughter to treat her mom?"

"Nope," said Nicole with a wink to Sunset.

"I'm glad you're here, actually," said Morgana. "Let's have some coffee and talk."

"When will Mark and Gary be here?" referring to the firm's two directors. They rarely worked together, but this desert shoot was complex, and both would be on duty.

"They're about half an hour away," said Sunset, checking the tracking app on her phone.

"Good," said Nicole. She sat on the table, legs swinging, sipping coffee from the red thermos Sunset had given to her. Looking at

Sunset, she said, "I love this vanilla-caramel mix you found. It's better than sex."

Sunset laughed. "Oh, come on. It can't be that good!"

Nicole smiled and nodded. "I've tried mixing it at home, but it didn't come out the same. Now I consider it my workday treat!"

"I'm glad. I need to talk to my mom for a bit."

"Sure."

Sunset and Morgana walked away for about five minutes. Nicole noticed them talking in hushed tones and caught Morgana looking back her way at one point. Something in the conversation bothered Nicole. It was not unusual for Sunset and Morgana, the mother-daughter team, to have private talks, but when on the set, this was unusual. Their body postures seemed to change, to stiffen, and they both turned and simultaneously started walking towards her.

Sensing the change in mood, Nicole stood and put down the coffee, which was nearly finished anyhow. "What's up, ladies?"

Morgana and Sunset stood before her. Morgana had a hand on her hip. Sunset had her arms crossed over her chest. Nicole was wary. They were both taking very aggressive postures.

"We've got a situation," said Morgana.

"So, uh, what's up?" asked Nicole.

"We need to advance you as an acolyte," said Morgana. "We need to get you to the next stage. There's some urgency now."

"Why?" she asked.

Sunset answered. She looked straight at Nicole, and Nicole felt like she was X-raying her to see her naked. Sunset said, "Because Gary Hart is coming for us."

"Oh?"

Nicole knew Gary Hart, of course. Everyone knew Gary Hart. But Nicole, via information from the Institute, knew of his TM background. Gary Hart was the founder and CEO of INN, the International News Network. Hart had started life as a TM but shifted to political power after founding INN in the 1970s. He was also a known acolyte of Quafara and Elkrod. He'd helped in their 2012 resurrection, and since they were banished back to hell in the Battle of Atlantia in 2015, he'd been working to bring them back. Unknown to all involved, in a few weeks, he would be killed in the attempt.

"We've got to be able to defend ourselves," said Morgana. "So we're going to push you today."

"How? I mean, I'm willing to do anything, you know that," said Nicole. She might well have been putting on her best acting performance, because she clearly was not willing to do anything.

"We haven't yet taught you the ultimate form of torture magic. Now is the time," said Sunset with a thin smile.

Nicole nodded. With a confidence she didn't feel, she snapped, "Sure. It's past due, if you ask me. How do we do that?"

Morgana stared. "We're going to turn Tabitha into a torture slave. She's not leaving here today. She's completely worthless and has no family or close friends. You need a source of power. She's it."

Nicole felt her body tense and the hairs on her neck raise. She could feel them watching her, sense their posture, wolves about to pounce on a rabbit if she ran for it.

There was no way she could beat the two of them in combat. It was questionable if she could even take down *one* of them.

She knew in her heart after finding her watch, the watch she'd had and 'lost' as a child as a trophy in Sunset's office on November 16 that they had killed her father, not Helena. She had been plotting to kill them, to take her vengeance, and was targeting a shoot before Christmas when just the three of them were scheduled. There would be no bystanders.

But her time had run out. And she was in far, far too deep to back out.

"Hey, that's good news," said Nicole.

"I'm glad you feel that way," said Sunset, putting a hand on Nicole's right shoulder. "We want the best for you."

"I appreciate that. You're excellent mentors. I knew you would be," said Nicole.

"I want to see Tabitha suffer, Nicole. I want her in *pain*. That's the only way to power up the first time. If you show mercy on her, it will weaken your channeling of the IM aural force," said Morgana.

Nicole nodded. "Got it. How do I start?"

"We're going to let Mark and Gary run the second unit with the other two girls. You're going to take Tabitha back to this horse trough set up behind cell five and we're going to torture her. You're going to convert that torture to pain."

"Okay. That sounds like fun," said Nicole convincingly. Hey, she was an actress by trade.

Sunset stared at Nicole. "I don't see enough anger in you, Stacy. Tabitha is a problem for us that must be *dealt* with."

"Dealt with?" asked Nicole, feeling her heart skip a beat. She knew damn well what Sunset meant.

"You know what I mean."

Nicole did, and she felt sick. But she just nodded.

"Use the hatred for the men that have abused you. Take it out on *her*. I know you don't like Tabitha."

"She's fucking annoying. She's an anchor," said Nicole, joining with the crowd.

"This is going to be *your* show. Impress us . . . or we may have to find others to serve us," said Morgana.

Nicole caught *everything* in that message — the tone, the posture, and the stare. She caught her breath. She knew it was quite clear that if they found others . . . Nicole *wouldn't* be breathing.

Nicole couldn't fight the two of them, not like this, not now. She didn't feel good. Satna Ana's always gave her a headache, but now her stomach hurt as well. Stress? Fear? Fuck, yes. *Fear*. She knew her life was on the line. She knew she couldn't beat the two of them in a fight. No chance.

"Ah, Tabitha is here."

They turned to see a beat up, twenty-year old, white Ford Ranger weaving across desert access road.

"Fuck, she's already loaded," said Morgana with a sigh.

"Mom, I'll get us ready," said Sunset.

"Good."

Nicole felt sick. She knew she was fighting for her life. If she played sick, if she made any move to resist, they'd suspect her and kill her.

Then Tabitha Tarasova arrived, parked, and walked slowly across the sand. She was twenty-three with a pretty face that had green, wide eyes, freckles, and a high forehead. She had curly blonde hair, very curly at the ends, more waves on the sides and top. She was buxom and cute when she wasn't hungover or high. Nicole had worked with her three times previously. The shoots were never smooth. There were always problems with Tabitha, because she was usually high, just like she was today.

"Heyyyyyy, baby," said Tabitha, her eyes rolling in her head and giggling.

"Shut the fuck up and get your clothes off. You're super-fucking late," said Sunset, slapping Tabitha's ass.

Nicole stood by as Morgana and Sunset quickly stripped Tabitha and tied her hands behind her back with a leather thong. Tabitha didn't giggle. She looked sad, about to cry.

"I get tied up all the time," she complained to Morgana.

Morgana slapped her. "Shut up."

Sunset then roughly dragged Tabitha to the horse trough, set up behind a fake wall. It was in the dirt. Tabitha was shoved to her knees and a ball gag put in her mouth.

As Nicole watched, she knew this was hopeless. She remembered the three times Tabitha had told her she wanted to kill herself. Nicole had once slipped her the suicide hotline. Tabitha had been abused throughout her teens. She had been in jail three times, two for solicitation and one for selling heroin. She had been beaten up many times and had a permanently chipped tooth and damaged hearing. She was covered in tattoos, mostly snakes and roses. She had permanent scars on her back from a whipping her stepfather had given her when she was thirteen. She had been sexually abused, physically abused, verbally abused, and had no family. Her father had abandoned her as a baby and her mother was in prison for murdering her boyfriend. Her friends were all drug users. She was only twenty-three.

Morgana turned to Nicole and whispered, "She's your victim now, acolyte. Make her *suffer*. Power up."

Nicole nodded and stood over Tabitha.

Then Nicole shoved Tabitha's head under the water, putting one hand on the back of her head and her left hand in the back between the shoulder blades. This pinned Tabitha's body between Nicole and the edge of the trough and, with Tabitha's hands bound behind her, she had no leverage at all to resist. She was helpless.

Feeling this helpless woman beneath her, Nicole felt an odd sense of power. TM surged through her. She was shocked at how powerful it was and how good it felt. All the warnings of its dangers from her friends and mentors, Doug and Sandy, at the Institute left her as she felt it's surge, like a rising orgasm.

But she felt *more* than that. She felt an overwhelming sadness for Tabitha, who was twenty-three and headed for an utter dead end of a life. She would wind up a slave to these monsters and suffer endlessly.

She had suffered enough.

Nicole kept holding Tabitha under. To Nicole's surprise, Tabitha didn't really struggle. She wiggled a bit but didn't make a desperate surge for escape.

Tabitha wanted to die.

Nicole helped her.

She kept holding Tabitha under, realizing she was going to kill her, to put her out of her misery. It was a mercy killing, for Tabitha was doomed. She was as doomed to live as a torture slave with Sunset and Morgana, a fate as fatal as if she had terminal cancer.

Sunset realized it had been too long, and she moved forward. But Morgana stopped her daughter, putting out a gentle restraining hand and gestured with a quick nod. Sunset stepped back and let it play out.

Nicole realized as Tabitha died beneath her hands what an intimate act murder truly was.

Tabitha soon stopped struggling, but Nicole held her under anyhow, unable to let go, absorbing a significant amount of TM.

Then she staggered back when Tabitha died, her aura leaving her body.

Nicole was utterly stunned.

She had just *murdered* someone.

"Stacy?" asked Morgana.

Nicole turned and stumbled away, her head spinning. She killed someone she killed someone she killed someone . . .

Sunset moved to follow but Morgana again stopped her. "She just murdered someone. Remember what it was like the first time?"

Cocking her head, Sunset nodded. "She needs a minute."

Nicole stumbled towards the catering area, her head splitting from a headache. She stumbled into a chair and put her head in her hands, the world spinning. She wanted to die.

After a few seconds, she sat up and . . . and was confused.

Why hadn't they started the shoot?"

Now Morgana approached.

Nicole asked, "Uh, where's Tabitha? When do we start?"

Morgana's eyes narrowed. Morgana had seen traumatic repression in action before and instantly recognized it. This wasn't anticipated, but was decidedly beneficial, so Morgana quickly said, "Uh . . . she called in sick. We're cancelling."

Sunset looked oddly at her mother but played along.

"Oh. Oh," said Nicole. Something felt wrong, but she didn't know what."

Morgana poured more of Nicole's favorite coffee. "Here take some for the road. Go home and rest."

And she did, oblivious to the fact that she now carried a killer inside.

Chapter Nine
The Pain of Memory

"AGHHHHHHHHHHHHHHHHHHHHHHHHHHHHHHHHHHHHHHH!" screamed Nicole as the memory flooded back. She writhed and twisted on the stretching rack, breaking bones in her ankles and wrists. She didn't feel any pain from the breaks.

Colie stepped back and started snapping her fingers. Two large earthworms that moved by sitting up on their coiled bottoms approached. One wore a tuxedo. The other wore a baseball home plate umpire's uniform. They both had yellowish skin, one eye, and looked worried.

"What's with her, boss?" asked the tuxedoed worm.

"Well, Thorg, the truth is not always kind. Make sure she doesn't escape," said Colie grimly.

Just as Colie finished her sentence, Nicole channeled with a fury of true rage . . . or perhaps insanity. The stretching rack vanished, and with a howl of rage, Nicole lunged at Colie. Nicole's nonsensical screams and babble came out so fast her words ran together almost incoherently.

The worms scrambled away. Nicole tackled Colie, oblivious to Colie's attempts to channel and keep Nicole at bay.

"Youdirteastingshitfacedmaggotlyingpisseatignwormthisdidn'thap ppennnnnnnnnnnnnnnnnnnnnnnnnnnnnn!"

Nicole had Colie pinned to the ground and began beating her face to a pulp. Colie cried out as her face was shattered, blood and bone flying everywhere. Colie couldn't stop Nicole.

"Scumsuckingpileofshitasslickingwhorekillyoukillyou!"

Nicole then grabbed a knife left behind by one of the fleeing worms and drove it so hard into Colie's throat that Colie was decapitated. Nicole kept hacking away as worms and flies flew out of Colie's, uh, corpse.

Nicole leapt to her feet, yanked off an arm, and began using the arm to beat the corpse to a pulp. In a fury that was almost beyond rage, she then channeled fire, which obviously was plentiful in Hell, and incinerated Colie.

Then she stepped back, breathing heavily, purely a psychological reaction as no one in Hell was physical and truly had to breathe. It was more a psychological catching of her breath.

"Got it out?"

Nicole whirled and was stunned to see the stretching rack had returned, and on it sat . . . Tabitha. She was nude, shaved, and wearing full make-up.

"You! No, this is a trick," said Nicole, raising her arms to channel.

Tabitha gestured and said, "Be calm."

Nicole instantly felt calm, calmer than she had ever felt before. Startled, she stepped back. She looked down to make sure she didn't trip over Colie's corpse . . . and realized it was gone.

She looked at Tabitha, who said, "It's really me, Nicole. I forgive you. I'm here to help you."

Nicole felt sick. She wanted to kill Tabitha, to eliminate the memory. "It isn't true. I didn't kill you."

"You did, my friend. You did it exactly as you remember," said Tabitha with great empathy and a shake of her head. "It's okay."

"AGHHHHHHHHHHHHHH!" screamed Nicole, and she threw her hands in the air, then collapsed to her knees and began hitting the rock.

Tabitha watched. Nicole beat the rock until her fingers and hands broke and were literally stumps on her hands. Nicole enjoyed the pain. She *deserved* the pain. It helped with the rage, and she deserved the punishment.

Finally, she was spent.

Tabitha said, "I'll heal your hands."

With a gesture, Tabitha sent forth energy and Nicole's hands were healed. Still on her knees, Nicole looked at them. They were fine. Even the nails were painted a deep red.

She looked up at Tabitha. "It's . . . true?"

"Yes, honey. You had to remember this to survive this mission. And to do the things that need to be done." She paused. "It's a lot to take in, I understand. Fortunately, in Hell, you have some time. I can adjust the time zone here. We can spend days, weeks, months on therapy to get you well before we resume the battle."

"Is it . . . I wanted to . . . I can't deal with this," said Nicole.

"You must!" said Tabitha urgently, joining Nicole on her knees, putting her hand son her shoulders. "You have no idea of the true stakes here."

"I know . . . Sam Grant sent me here."

"Because you can do the job. And my partner here, well, we know you're who we needed. Sam sent you here for a reason."

Suddenly puzzled, Nicole cocked her head. "How did you know Sam sent me here?"

Tabitha smiled. "Baby, we . . . my partners and I . . . we were behind Sam calling you. We can touch his subconscious in dreams, and while in his coma he is particularly susceptible to . . . suggestion."

Nicole nodded. That made sense, at least as much as anything made sense in Hell. "I . . . I'm sorry."

"I know. And *that's important*," said Tabitha, helping Nicole to her feet. "You have true repentance. But we must work through it."

Nicole looked around. They were suddenly in a therapist office that was oddly in black and white. All the furniture was zebra patterned and there were no walls. All the books were in shelves, and the wood was an off-white.

"Uh, what happened to Colie?" Nicole asked.

Tabitha cocked her head and smiled gently. "Nicole . . . you didn't figure it out?"

"I'm not in the mood for games," said Nicole irritably.

"*I* was Colie."

Nicole's eyes widened and she stepped back. The carpet was actually fingers, and they grabbed Nicole's feet and held her in place.

"It's okay," said Tabitha with a smile. "I had to appear in a form you would trust, and you trust no one but yourself."

"That's not true."

"it is true. It's why you weren't part of Ops, why you left the Institute, why you lived alone. Oh, you have other good reasons, the trauma and such, but at the end of all of it, you don't trust anyone. The only person you would trust is yourself — hence your future self came to guide you."

Nicole shook her head. "This is . . . weird."

Tabitha nodded. "Well, it wasn't fun being dismembered and pummeled with my own arm, but I expected it — and such things happen quite a bit here in Hell." She shook her head. "I've been here since my death, Nicole, but even those of us in Hell are not always . . . condemned. There is redemption. There is change. And you must help us with it."

"I don't understand . . . you should hate me. I killed you."

Tabitha looked sad, very sad, very distant, and like a child. "Oh, Nicole, I was dead long before you finished me off. I was using drugs regularly, I was HIV positive, which is why I was doing those idiotic snuff films — I couldn't have sex. You know some of my life. There's more. My father abused me, my mother hated me, my best friend was a neighbor who was also a cop who let me come to his house when my parents had drunken fights. In return for hand jobs, I had TV and food. That was my life." She paused. "But I also made a mess of it. I gave up. I didn't try to get better, and in that, I hurt other people. I knew I was positive and fucked my boyfriend anyhow. I knew and shared needles with others. I killed many more people than you — five, I'm told." She laughed with the borderline giggle of the perilously close to insane. "They keep *very good* statistics here. There are entire fiefdoms of Hell that crunch numbers."

"I'm . . . I don't know what to say," said Nicole, feeling emotionally spent. "Other than I'm sorry."

"That's really all you need to say," said Tabitha.

"How can I help?"

Tabitha smiled. "How do you feel?"

"I feel . . . overwhelmed." She hit her chest with a fist. "But I came to Hell knowing this would be the ultimate trial, knowing the stakes. As . . . as *disgusted* with myself as I am . . . as angry as I am . . . I'm shutting it off. I'll deal with it later. I'll punish myself later."

"You will have to grieve when you return to life . . . assuming you make it. You know that, right?" asked Tabitha.

"I know," said Nicole with grim resignation.

"You also know . . . if you hadn't done that, Sunset and Morgana, they would have killed you on the spot."

"I know. That isn't an excuse. I was a coward. But I'll deal with penance later. I must . . . no matter what . . . complete my mission here. I take it you know about it?"

Tabitha nodded. "Nicole . . . my friend . . . and you are my friend, even if you did kill me . . . my friend had a lot to do with getting you here."

"Friend?"

"You don't know her," said Tabitha. "But we should meet. Ready for a trip?"

Nicole held out her hand. "Yes. But I must promise you, when this is over, we must redeem your soul."

Tabitha smiled. "I think our mission will take care of this."

"How do we travel?"

"We don't. This is the end of my role. There's a team of us helping with this operation . . . but don't fear. You'll be back with your friends and just where you need to be. Fred will take you the rest of the way."

"Okay. I'm . . . I can't just leave you."

"You aren't. Have faith, Nicole. It is your only weapon here."

Nicole nodded. "I don't understand the things that have happened to me or that I have done, but I have faith God has reasons. His ways are not our ways. Very well. What do I do?"

Tabitha made a request of Nicole to be carried out when Nicole returned to life. Then she said. "It's easy, my friend. Just shut your eyes and hold my hands. It's like clicking your heels three times."

Chapter Ten
Advance on Hitler

"Three times I done said this," muttered Tripper with disgust, staring at the gigantic river of boiling human fat that barred their path.

"And we heard you the *first* time," muttered Lisa.

"Then gimme an answer," said Tripper with disgust, throwing his baseball cap down on the floorboard of his yellow racing car.

The six members were split across four cars. They were like the electronic racing cars teenage boys set up in their basements, running along electronic tracks and racing to beat trains. Tripper was alone in a yellow car, because it was tiny. He was folded up like a spider. In a red car, Geneva drove and leaned back on Krissy's lap, and in a blue car, Lisa drove and leaned back on Sherry's lap, sort of like riders at an amusement park. And like Tripper, Dirk was in his own car, his white with a blue racing stripe.

They were on a road made of brain matter of cows. The road came to a dip, and the dip was flooded with the boiling fluid. Tripper had parked, asking Lisa what to do. She just stared. He threw a piece of cow brain matter into the river, where it was burned as if by acid instantly. He again asked Lisa what to do. She just shrugged. So, he asked the third time, which got her sassy reply.

At least she was talking.

Geneva said, "Tripper, I don't think she knows what to do."

"I don't," said Lisa. "This isn't supposed to be here."

"That's very true," said Sherry.

"It appears the jig is up, old friend," said Dirk to Tripper.

Tripper looked both ways, and the river passed into the horizon. They were in a valley of volcanic mountains, with scattered trees that were really people burning on crosses. It smelled, it was hot, and it was loud, and it was getting on Tripper's nerves.

"Well, reckon we can't go around it or through it, so usin' decades of my deductive skilled honed by running my own agency, I say we gotta go *over* it."

"Brilliant. How?" snapped Lisa.

"That's your job, I reckon. Y'all is the native," said Tripper.

Krissy said to Lisa, "Aw, just ignore him. He's always a jerk when he can't figure something out."

"Aren't all men?"

Geneva's car was to Tripper's right, and she backed up and parked between the other two cars and said, "What's past the river?"

Sherry said, "Hell's geography is a little complicated. The place generally breaks into the nine levels Dante outlined centuries ago. But there's nooks and crannies all over the place, and this is one of them. Past that river is Nazi Germany, part of the ninth circle now. That's where Hitler is stationed, planning his takeover."

"So we gotta get there," said Tripper with resolve.

"Hell is mental. Can't we just turn these cars into helicopters and fly over?" asked Geneva.

Lisa shrugged. "If we're strong enough mentally."

"Well . . . there may be those that oppose us as well," said Dirk.

"Getting' a little squeamish?" asked Tripper with a chuckle.

"I have seen the horrors of the ninth level. It is not a joke," said Dirk seriously.

"We must fly. Let's focus and do it," said Geneva confidently.

Geneva's car suddenly grew wings like those on a wasp and her car lifted into the air. Lisa and Sherry quicky followed. Tripper was next. Then Krissy. Dirk was last.

"Lot cheaper than Delta!" shouted Geneva.

"Don't seem to be any problems," said Tripper.

Suddenly, they were being shot at by lasers from science-fiction UFO crafts, literally bowls of steel. Tripper shouted, "Focus on a shield!"

The team was able to block all the lasers, all but Dirk. He was dislodged from his car when the floor was blown out. He screamed as he fell into the river of bile.

"Well, reckon he's outta the ball game," muttered Tripper.

Lisa said, "That won't kill him. It'll just zap him back to where he was."

They flew through fog on the other side of the bile river. Suddenly, there was a clearing, and in a valley was a huge German castle.

"Let's land and walk," said Geneva.

"Agreed," said Tripper.

They landed, then walked about five miles to approach a courtyard near the castle, which otherwise was surrounded by tree trunks that were really the backbones of cowards. Cautiously, they studied the mammoth structure, which looked like something from medieval times.

"Why aren't there guards?" asked Geneva warily.

Lisa answered. "Hitler generally doesn't need guards. He can pretty much dispatch anyone here while picking his nose. But I'm sure there's a few scattered about, so be careful."

"We gotta go this way," said Tripper, pointing with his cane.

"How on Earth — or I guess more appropriately, how the Hell do you know that?" asked Geneva.

"This castle is a replica of the one where me and your grandpappy cornered Hitler and killed him at the end of the Big One. Ain't like I could ever forget that place."

"You killed Hitler? I never knew that," said Krissy.

"I thought people in Hell would know everything," muttered Tripper, only half paying attention, focused on studying the castle.

"Well, we do, sort of. But only things we *want* to know about. No one ever told me, but then again, I never asked. I asked if you were happy and stuff like that . . . you were a good man, Tripper."

"I still am, I hope," said Tripper with a chuckle. "We'll see how this shit all plays out."

"There's someone coming," whispered Geneva. They backed against the stone wall that ringed the grass courtyard that surrounded the castle. The trees sheltered them. Perhaps the most striking thing about the castle and property was the fact that it seemed genuine. The grass was grass, the trees were trees, the stones were stones, not some sort of twisted, grotesque abomination of human or animal flesh.

"Good . . . uh, sumbitch," said Tripper. He almost used the word 'Lord,' remembering at the last instant the instant shocks any condemned suffered in Hell for uttering that word.

"You know him?" asked Geneva, seeing the shock on Tripper's face.

"That is one mean motherfucker," said Tripper, whispering to Geneva.

"A TM?"

"Yeah. His name is Hans Heinz."

"Are you kidding?"

"Nope. He was one of Hitler's inner cadre of TM agents. We took him out on the way in . . . Anne actually killed his ass, dropped a chandelier on him. Anne always hated two things, Nazis and chandeliers," he said, smiling at the thought of his late wife, who passed away from cancer decades ago. "Look, he's calling over the guards."

They watched for a moment. Hans paused by the drawbridge as the two Nazi guards approached. Both were young; one with short blond hair, another bald. Both were fit and white, of course. Hans gave them instructions that Tripper couldn't hear from his vantage point. Then the two guards began to remove their clothes.

"Uh, oh. We're gonna get X-rated," said Krissy.

"Hold on a bit. We can use it as a distraction."

They waited as the bald guard fell to his knees in the grass. Hans then unzipped his fly and kneeled behind the man. Soon, he penetrated him, creating a yelp from the man which they did hear.

The other two guards dropped to hands and knees, obviously preparing for their inevitable turn.

Geneva looked at Tripper. "I thought Nazis hated homosexuality?"

"Yup. Don't mean there weren't some of 'em with ol' Adolf. Besides, this is Hell. May well be a punishment for them."

Geneva nodded. "Valid point."

"Let's move round right. There's a window into the second bedroom. He won't hear us while he's busy with them."

"Agreed," said Geneva.

They quickly crossed the yard. Geneva approached the window, which didn't have glass. It was just open space, about two feet off the ground and fairly large, easily large enough for a person to enter.

Geneva looked at Tripper. "I don't sense any alarms, physical or paranormal. This seems awful easy. I don't care how powerful you are, you don't let someone walk into your house unimpeded."

Tripper nodded. "I know, but I reckon we ain't got no choice but to play it out."

Sherry suddenly said, "This could be an indicator Hitler is about to make his move. Even in Hell — look, Hell is just like anywhere. Resources aren't unlimited. He may have pulled back all unnecessary aspects of the realm to conserve power for the big moment."

"Lot of guessin' in that," said Tripper reluctantly, rubbing his beard.

Geneva stared into the room. It was a bedroom, but mostly a storage room. While there was a bed and a nightstand, the rest of the room was full of crates. She looked back at the others and said, "Do we go in?"

"I'll go first. If it's a trap, it's me or y'all that he wants, not the others. We might well as shit get it sprung."

Geneva moved into position to cover Tripper. The other three women stepped well back, though still along the wall to avoid being spied upon by Heinz were he to finish his recreation with the guards.

Tripper entered. His gangly, daddy long-legs form didn't make for a smooth entry. He looked around, shrugged, and headed for a large oak door ahead. He opened the door. He looked around, then returned to the others.

"Well?" asked Geneva impatiently.

"Reckon I heard distant voices. This end seems unused, musty, wasn't no one about. There's a corridor that leads toward the center. Are we in?"

Everyone more or less shrugged. Only Geneva said firmly, "Very well."

"I'll lead," said Tripper.

They stealthily entered the room, then approached the door. Tripper led them into the corridor, which was about ten feet tall and several feet wide, much larger than a corridor in a conventional house. The ceiling was curved into the wall, and all the doors had an arch shape. Flaming torches lit their way.

"You're right, it doesn't smell like anyone has been down here in years," whispered Geneva.

"Yeah. Reckon we got lucky at last."

That's when Tripper stepped on a loose stone.

They all vanished.

"Owwwwww," muttered Geneva, rolling onto her right side. "Tripper?"

She opened her eyes, hoping she hadn't hurt her right elbow when she fell after Tripper stumbled, and suddenly realized she was in big trouble.

"Welcome, Miss Kane."

"You. *You filthy pig*," snarled Geneva with unusual venom.

Before her on a throne sat a nude David Mize. This was Mize as she had known him in 2006, when he was fifty-seven years old. He was a stocky man, short but squat, sturdy, built like a series of boxes. His square torso supported an equally square head, a source of great amusement for many childhood tormentors. Piggish eyes glared out from beneath thick glasses that had square, black frames like those issued by the military or a prison. His greasy black hair was cut short and uncombed. Geneva thought that Mize was damn ugly, but ugly in an intimidating and not an endearing manner. He was no longer in reasonable shape, now quite fat. Oh, and he was erect.

She thought that he was the type of man who could walk into a chatting crowd and instantly silence them. Not that he was being overtly mean or even acting particularly angry at the moment. He was just able to suck the energy out of anything.

As for the throne, it was made of a mesh of human tendons, sort of like a lawn chair. It sat on a field of grass that wasn't grass but human fingers. They whined as they were stepped on.

Geneva moved towards him aggressively, suddenly wearing some type of futuristic, gold body armor. Her body glowed yellow and purple, typical aural shading for probability cloud channeling or manifestations.

She despised Mize, who had taken her captive in 2006 and hooked her to his machine that used her life-force in a failed attempt to control the probability cloud created when Jennifer Saunders was turned into a soul survivor in Arizona in 2004. He had stripped her, other than her boots, bound her, and turned her into an object, a tool for his own power. He had rendered her helpless, a lesson not lost on her. She escaped thanks to the boots, which she used to ground the machine and divert the PC power.

"I'm going to turn you into a baby octopus and step on you," she hissed and moved forward.

But then she stopped. This wasn't her, this was Hell pulling out her innermost anger. She had to control herself.

She was better than this. She was not some woman scorned. She was here for a greater purpose.

Mize just glared at her with a stone face. Finally, when he realized she wasn't going to advance, he said, "I could have been a god."

"No, because you're a petty imbecile. If I hadn't stopped you, someone would have," said Geneva bluntly.

He frowned. "That's . . . likely. I didn't have an easy life."

"I don't care. I don't have time."

"Everyone wants you down here, you know. You're a bigger prize than a winning lottery ticket. But . . . I just don't care. I don't much care about anything anymore."

"I have places to go."

"It wasn't easy being me," he said. "I was raised in Dayton in the fifties and sixties. I was physically and sexually abused by my father, you know. He was a cold man. My mother was always depressed." His voice had no inflection. "I got sent to Vietnam, got turned into a vampire. Bill taught me about TM. Then he died. Then . . . I don't remember anything after that blonde woman buried me in the flash flood. I just remember water . . . I could have been a different person. Everything was stacked against me."

She wasn't getting sucked into his story of self-pity or using her empathy. This was Hell. It was too late to help him, and besides, she figured this was a trap. "I don't have time for this. I'm leaving."

"But you don't know the way out," he said with a sly smile, the first real movement and emotion he had shown.

Now she paused . . . studied him . . . and laughed.

"Of course, I do, you stupid pig. Farewell."

And suddenly, she slowly faded away, then vanished.

"Dad!" shouted Lisa in shock.

"Lisa! Gol'dang! My, you're lookin' good! Where's your sis?"

"I'm not sure. Hold on, dad!" she shouted.

Big Jack McGrath was in a wing of a prison cell. The entire prison was bone and tendons. There didn't seem to be any other prisoners. Big Jack was naked and fat, this being a manifestation of him just before his death.

Lisa found some loose bone on the floor made of hardened molten lava and pried open the bars, allowing Big Jack to step through. "Good work, li'l woman."

"Thanks, dad."

Sherry suddenly arrived, nude and clearly aroused. She leaned against the door that led to the next wing and assumed a sultry pose. "Yeah, rescues are so sexy."

Lisa smiled. She loved Sherry's body. The two half-sisters met in '07 when Lisa was fifteen and Sherry sixteen. Lisa and her mother had moved to Dallas from Newport Beach a year earlier. Lisa never forgot their first meeting at Big Jack's home. When Lisa saw Sherry, it was literally love at first sight. It was the same for Sherry. The two of them locked eyes, and in that moment, they were bound for life, sexual partners and partners in all things.

Big Jack said, "Go on, honey, you freed me. That earns you street cred, as they say these days. Go on and celebrate."

Somewhere, Lisa knew this was . . . not what they were here for. But since arriving in Hell, she and Sherry had been banned from their incestuous lovemaking, the punishment for executing such actions on Earth.

Sherry stared at Lisa.

Lisa stared at Sherry.

They started to move towards each other . . . but then they stopped.

They turned to their father.

"What the hell, girls?"

"We won't do this. We're here . . . to help Tripper. We're here to save our souls, father," said Sherry.

"We might have done evil acts on Earth, but we aren't evil. Little Jack gave us a chance to change. We're taking it."

Big Jack suddenly threw up his hands and started jumping up and down like a child having a fit over a broken toy. "Damn you women! You've ruined everything!"

Then he turned into a bowl of porridge.

"Whoa," said Lisa. Sherry just stared in shock.

Suddenly, they saw a man with red skin, horns, hooves, and a barrel chest stomping towards them. Satan, in traditional garb.

"Uh, oh," said Sherry.

But he didn't attack. Instead, shaking his head, he said, "Gotta give it to you, ladies, you pulled off the upset of the century down here."

"Huh?" asked Lisa.

"No one thought you'd resist the temptation. There were million to one odds out there! Some gamblers are gonna lose fingers and toes." Then he laughed. "Of course, this is Hell. That shit happens every day."

The women backed away but backed into the corridor. "What . . . what does this mean?"

"You won. You get your souls back — and in this case, that means getting your *life* back. It's the terms of agreement when there's this type of situation. I'd explain, but then I'd need fifty lawyers and about sixteen years."

"We're . . . going back to life?"

"Yep. Enjoy."

He snapped his fingers, and they were gone.

Satan looks around. "Shit, this damn building always moves around. I gotta get maps. Which way do I go to get back?"

"You're lost again?"

Krissy turned abruptly, surprised she was in a hotel in Tampa Bay, and surprised that it apparently was 1979 again. Well, and surprised she was naked.

The man talking to her was someone she knew. He was tall with blond hair parted in the middle, a big jaw, cold blue eyes, and a smirk. He had a sort of roguish physical appeal. He was once in good shape, but now a little fat.

"Dennis," said Krissy. "Where am I? We were in Hitler's castle."

"Oh, I got you out of there. That was a losing deal," he said, and he took out a package and threw it to her.

Cocaine.

Krissy shut her eyes and winced. "Get away from me."

"You don't want that."

She was on her knees on a carpet of writhing maggots, the image of the room slowly fading into the reality of Hell, such as it was. Krissy knew nothing but the bag of coke. In the late 1970s, she was in her thirties and her life was going nowhere fast. She got involved with a cult called the Saints of Diego. They were really just a group assembled to try and legalize coke, and they turned her into a raging cokehead. After spending four years doing just about anything humanly possible for a fix, she wound up in rehab after she was riding in a car that crashed. That sort of got her back on track. She gave up the coke. But she never really got her life back on track.

Krissy died in 1996 of a heart attack, her heart finally giving out due to damage from her coke years.

"I do want that," she said. The furniture was melting like butter, becoming its true form, bone. And in the far corner was a lamp made from an Orthomayer, an alien from Cygnus Beta that looked like an anteater.

"No, you don't. Stay here, baby. When Tripper and his team fail, Satan will punish those that helped him. You don't want that."

Krissy cried.

Dennis approached. He had been one of her prime sources, a coke peddler for eleven years until he was killed in a shootout with police in Pacific Palisades at an Arby's. He was a busy man in Hell. A man that could move product was popular in any dimension.

"Don't cry, Krissy," he said, throwing out another bag. "This is good stuff, and you can't OD here. A hit of this and you'll be happy for decades."

Krissy said, "No . . . I have to help Tripper. I have to . . . he believed in me."

Dennis smiled and shook his head. "Honey . . . he zapped away and left you here."

She was shocked. "No. He wouldn't. I'm going to go see him."

She tried to push past him to the door. But the door wouldn't open. Whirling, she said, "Let me out."

Before she could move, he jumped her, putting a hand over her mouth and forcing her to snort the coke.

Krissy struggled, but the instant she had the coke in her, the smells and sensations came back . . . the memories of how she felt under the drug, so good, like a fucking goddess.

Slowly, she slipped to the rug.

She wallowed on it, snorting the coke from the packs . . . and the floor slowly rose and sucked her back to her permanent station in Hell. And she didn't care. The pleasure of the cocaine high was strong, and it had been so, so long since she had been to paradise.

"Been a while since I done been here," muttered Tripper.

He was leaning against a stone wall, looking around a curving corner in Hitler's castle. This wasn't the replica, but the actual castle from '45.

The details were what those not in the war missed when they watched films. The low, consistent rumble of cannons, like thunder in the distance. The smell of smoke, death, fear, and sweat. The taste of blood and bile.

He rounded the corner, cane at the front, expecting an attack. None came. He reached a set of double doors, like those for waiters at restaurants. Grunting, he pushed through, realizing he had little choice but to play out this sequence. He had a very unpleasant feeling their trip to find Hitler had been intercepted.

Inside, the room was a chemical lab. In the corner tied to a metal support pole, hands over her head, was Anne Hinkle-Heinrich. She was a classic blonde on blue beauty who had a movie star profile, the type that was gorgeous even in a black and white movie. That was her main feature, as she was very slim and flat elsewhere, like a runner.

Anne was wearing a gestapo output, the jacket ripped off and the pants ripped, which told Tripper this was sometime before the invasion against Hitler, when Anne was working undercover. She was also gagged with duct tape, her eyes wide with fear. She struggled as she saw Tripper, clearly alarmed, but communicating with her eyes.

Working at a lab table near her with bubbling vials of chemicals was a man Tripper instantly recognized. He was a very tall, gangly man with curly brown hair, a big nose, dark eyes with large circles under them, big ears, and acne scars that were mostly hidden under a beard. He was six-six and awkward, as if he were a teen that had grown too fast, but the man was twenty-six. Or at least he looked 26 to Tripper, who only knew this man when he was 26.

This man was Omega, also known as Bobby Brunner of Brooklyn.

Omega was wearing a black hoodie, jeans, and sneakers. Anne was streaked red and purple by shallow cuts and whip marks.

Tripper was wary. "Omega?"

"O'Sullivan. *About time* you made your way to Hell. It's long overdue." He adjusted an ancient radio and *Hornpipe* by Handle began to play, drowning out the background of gunfire and the screams of the dying. The smell of death was still prevalent.

Tripper slowly nodded, slowly moving to the right. The room was windowless and had no other exits, but he wanted a better line of fire at Omega, who was cross-corner from the door and thus mostly shielded by the lab tables.

Alarmingly, Tripper felt his bones starting to hurt badly. It was getting hard just to stand, and he leaned on his cane. As he did so, Omega gave a half smile. "It has been a long time, O'Sullivan."

Tripper nodded. After all, it had.

In the waning days of the war, a team of paranormals were assembled by the government to make a raid on Hitler. Tripper joined Golden Bear, Gerald Kane, Anne Hinkle-Heinrich, and Omega. Anne, Gerald, and Omega were taken down by the defenses around Hitler's bunker. But that allowed Tripper and Golden Bear to reach Hitler. Tripper was badly hurt, but he broke down Hitler's defenses, which allowed Golden Bear to break through and impale Hitler on a bronze flagpole.

The battle was costly for Tripper, who broke forty bones. As a teenager, he had been infused with zombie magic during his battle against the Trouts. That enabled him to heal much of it, but from that point forward, he was held together mostly by sheer willpower and the fear of dying and facing Hell and Caroline, facing that failure.

The team split up. Gerald returned to Maine and started his comic book career. Golden Bear returned to Russia a hero, which he still was. Tripper and Anne returned to the States. Anne was originally from Chicago, but they retired to Tripper's home in Tupelo. They had worked together during the war several times, she being a double-agent for the Allies. She was a widow, her husband being killed in a battle in Asia trying liberate prisoners of Japanese camps near Singapore in 1944.

They were married for fifteen years, during which time Tripper healed. They had a small home by the Tombigbee waterway. They lived peacefully until Anne died of brain cancer in 1960, something Tripper was certain, though having no evidence of it, was caused by exposure to chemicals during the war.

TM activity was light after the war, which had drained paranormal resources around the world. It wasn't until Kelkirk and Zenith moved to New York in the late 1950s that paranormal activity began to ramp up. After Anne died in '60, Tripper founded his Tricky Dick Detective Agency, using it as a cover to create a network of contacts to help him stop torture magicians. And he began to travel. Increased mobility was making it harder to track TMs, as they no longer were localized.

"I heard y'all retired to South America, to hunt the Nazis that escaped," said Tripper to Omega. He could tell by Anne's eye movements that she wanted him to keep Omega talking.

"Yes . . . yes." Omega glared and held a vial. "There is a lethal acid in his vial I invented. If I splash it on your woman, she'll be consumed before you can save her."

Tripper caught Anne's eye movements and rubbed his right ear, something that looked like a nervous twitch but actually was a way to indicate to Anne that he understood her message.

"Omega, I don't get it. You're our friend."

Omega laughed a laugh on the borderline of hysteria and insanity. He then pointed at Tripper and said, "I cared nothing for you, fool! You or your wench."

He turned and slapped Anne.

Tripper held his position but used the distraction to subtly move his cane's position.

"I wanted Hitler's power, hillbilly! The entire objective of aiding you and your morons was to weaken Hitler enough to steal his power."

"Steal?"

"Drain his aura."

Tripper shook his head. "Spells like that are damn hard and need help. Reckon that was way beyond your ability."

He glared. "Don't insult me. I was on the verge, but was taken out by Snartooth, you may recall. After the war, I wanted the power. I relocated to South America and worked with many Nazis that fled. But on an attempt to secure a rare and valuable totem in an Aztec temple in '56, I was killed." He waved his hands around. "And here I remain."

"Right so, I reckon," said Tripper, a little saddened his old friend had such a cold agenda. But they had never maintained contact after the war, something Tripper knew had to have been instigated by Omega and probably wasn't a good sign.

"I've waited for so long to get one of you back. Now I have both!"

Tripper was puzzled by this comment but didn't let him distract him. "Y'all ain't got shit but a case of bad ego!"

Instantly, he hurled the cane like a club, hitting Omega in the face, knocking him backwards and into an electrical device. It lit up and fried him. He screamed and melted into a puddle.

Tripper quickly released Anne and said, "Gol' damn . . . it really is *you*! I can sense your aura."

Anne smiled, hugged him, and kissed him. They were both instantly young and in love again. For Tripper, it was one of the best moments of his life . . . for Anne, one of the best moments of her post-life.

Finally, she broke the embrace and said, "I love you. I've missed you."

"Reckon so, reckon I feel the same. How are you here?"

She smiled wickedly. "I am a double-agent. That was my specialty in the war, and it's working now."

"But who are you working for?" he asked, completely confused.

"Heaven, of course. Come, we must move as we talk. Hitler is close to commencing his efforts, which will be cataclysmic."

"Right."

He followed her out the door, back into Hitler's castle. Anne said, "Move quickly, but warily. I fell for a trap, which was how Omega snared me."

"How can . . . reckon I don't get it."

She said hurriedly, "I know. I don't know details either. I'm in a 'need to know' situation. I'm paying my role, which was to make sure you and Geneva get to the final battle. You're essential." She paused and said sadly. "I'm sorry, love, but Krissy won't make it. She surrendered to the temptations of Hell."

Tripper nodded sadly. "I had hope for Krissy. But it is what it is. She has chosen her path."

"The McGrath sisters have been redeemed and are back on Earth, so they can't help us any longer."

He rolled his eyes. "Reckon that'll shake LJ up a bit! Gotta admit, I never did think those crazy broads would make it. Glad they did, though."

Anne hugged him. "You're a good man. Come on."

They ran as Anne finished explaining as they approached large double-doors once again. "All I know is Heaven is actually in danger if Hitler takes control of Hell. Like Hell, Heaven is just a blank slate dimension. It can be . . . altered."

"Altered? Then why ain't the big guy himself here? I've heard he comes and tries to rescue the lost here from time to time."

"I don't know. He's letting it play out, something like that."

"Reckon this door is it?" he asked, as they had stopped before the door.

"Yes. I can go no further, and time is now important. But I have time to tell you that the best moments of my life were our walks along the river with the dogs."

Then she kissed him.

"I will be waiting, dear," she said.

Then she slowly vanished, her smile last, like a Cheshire cat.

Tripper immediately turned to the door, because he had to either fight or cry. He pushed it inwards.

"Tripper!" shouted Geneva as he suddenly appeared beside her, walking through the doors into her corridor.

"Gol'dang, reckon that was a gamble that done paid off," he muttered, hugging his old friend.

"I fought Mize and realized I could just leave, go anywhere, if I put aside my hatred and showed forgiveness. It worked. Movement here is mental."

"Reckon I did more or less the same," he said, not wanting to talk about Anne. He would tell Geneva later. "Uh, I got info, Krissy and the girls, they won't be joining us. But we should be in place to fight the big guy."

Geneva smiled. "No matter what happens, I appreciate your efforts and I love you. Just . . . as a friend."

"Reckon I rightly feel the same. Gerald would be proud as shit of you."

"He would," she said with a cute smile. "I'm sorry about Krissy."

"We can't all be winners," said Tripper sadly.

They were presently in Hitler's castle at the end of a dead-end corridor that had no other doors. Directly ahead was a door made of bone with a doorhandle and a big sign saying:

ENTER TO VISIT SATAN. NO APPOINTMENT NECESSARY.

Tripper but his hand on the doorhandle. "Ready?"
She nodded. "Let's see what the Big Man's got."

Chapter Eleven
Sylvester and the Ninth Circle

"Is this the right bridge?" asked Sparrow with doubt.

No one said anything. After giving explanations, Hart had led the team of himself, Trixie, Tripper, Gwen, Lancelot, Sparrow, and Kress to this area of Hell.

They stared, stunned. They stood before a rope bridge with wooden slats that extended over a bottomless valley, the walls lined with blood. The valley looked like the esophagus of a hippopotamus. The rope was really tendons of the dead, and the boards their flattened bodies. It sagged considerably and had to be a quarter of a mile long.

Finally, Hart said, "Well, Lance?"

"Your guidance was true. It is the path to the Ninth Circle, as it exists now."

"It smells like a toilet that hasn't been cleaned since 1972," said Kress.

Sylvester ignored her. The wind made it noisy, and the sky was red and hot. He said, "Lancelot, what challenges will we face?"

"I know not. None have dared cross this bridge since it was installed after Hitler's arrival in 1945."

Sylvester shrugged. "Well, I see little alternative. Who is with me?"

Hart held up his drink. "From this point forward, this is a battle. There is nothing Trixie and I can do. Only you can stop Hitler, Sylvester. That's the way it works."

Sylvester merely nodded slowly. Hart was telling him something subtly under the banter, and Sylvester understood it. In fact, Sylvester already knew it.

Smiling, Hart added, "Good luck, old man. We'll wait for you here."

"Yeah, we'll guard your back," said Trixie.

Sylvester chuckled. "Such bravery!"

"I'm in. Let's get this over with," said Kress.

"I will lead us," said Lance.

"And I am with you," added Gwen.

Sylvester looked at Sparrow. "You?"

"I haven't had this much amusement since I got here. The chance to see you laid up in the Ninth Circle is definitely worth a walk," said Sparrow, then she laughed manically.

"Very well."

The five of them started across the bridge.

Hart turned to Trixie. "Well, I think that's the end of that. There's really no reason to stay. They'll win or lose, live or die, and nothing will change for us, I suspect. Care to visit the horse races?"

"Sure. I could do with seeing some cheating husband run with a horse carriage attached to his ass. I'm sure we'll never hear from these idiots again. At least we got paid well to get them here."

"Alas, it was quite entertaining. I must admit, I'm surprised. I thought Sylvester would wise up and quit."

"Again, I ask is this wise?" said Kress.

The bridge was very unstable. The wind ripped at it as if alive, trying to pull them off it. The bottom was endless. The walls were bleeding. But the worst was the screams of the souls they were stepping on as they moved across the bridge.

"It is the only choice," said Sylvester.

"That doesn't answer the question."

"Be silent, wench!" shouted Gwen, turning and putting her sword under Kress' chin.

Kress shut up.

Sylvester frowned. "We must press on."

They did so, despite winds that were stronger than the strongest of hurricanes. Only their willpower kept them moving. But eventually, they were paralyzed, only about two-thirds of the way across the bridge.

Sparrow looked at Sylvester. "We . . . can't . . . can't make it."

"We must!"

Sparrow looked at the others. Then she said to Kress. "You have the ability to portal."

"Yeah, with a brand."

"Grab your master, woman," said Sparrow, grabbing Kress's wrist.

"Hey, he most certainly is not my fucking master," said Kress, noticing Sylvester staring absently ahead.

"Prepare to take him. Take his right hand."

Sylvester turned and reached out. Kress grabbed his wrist. Gwen and Lance were pinned to the bridge by the winds.

"You two must go. You must succeed," said Sparrow, looking at Sylvester.

"How?"

Sparrow's hand turned to fire. "I've learned tricks over the years."

Kress's eyes widened. "Oh, no. I'm not going to have you brand me, you fucking nut!"

But Kress then screamed as Sparrow simply grabbed Kress' right thigh.

"Fare you well, Sylvester. We'll talk again soon if you succeed," said Sparrow.

Then Sylvester and Kress vanished.

The bridge split apart, sending Gwen, Lance, and Sparrow downward into the abyss, screaming forever . . . until they finally lost their voices.

"Can you hear me?" Kress whispered.

Sylvester nodded. "Aye."

"Where are we?" she whispered.

"Be silent."

They were staring at a spotlight on a white, wooden chair sitting on an empty theatre stage.

"You're irritable," hissed Kress.

"Can you not sense the evil?" he asked, glaring at her.

She shrugged.

Then a man materialized in a haze of light on stage. He looked a bit like a skinny Santa Claus: old with a long, white beard, hair, and wrinkles, but a twinkle in the eye. He wore a long, purple robe that had yellow stars on it.

"Sylvester Starnes. Your arrival is . . . as expected."

"I thought as much. I am coming to terms with the end game."

"Who's he?" whispered Kress.

"Away, child," said the man, and he gestured forward, waving his hand.

"Heyyyyyyyyyyyyyyyyyyyyyyyyyyyyyyyyy!" shouted Kress, her voice fading.

"Whumpffffffffffffff!" she muttered as she opened her eyes to see she was in the lab in St. Martin.

She looked around, utterly stunned. "What the . . . Hell?"

Starting to get up, she suddenly froze, realizing she was still on the table and therefore any movement out of position could disrupt the spell. That means she was stuck there until the others woke up.

Throwing her head back, she muttered, "Fuck me. I've pissed myself and I'm hungry and now I'm stuck here until they get back home."

Grimly, she realized they might never get back home. Or it might be a long time. They had never considered that one of them might return *prior* to the completion of the mission.

She was trapped on the table in the lab. Even if she didn't care about the others, and admittedly she had mixed feelings towards them, disrupting the spell would incinerate her in psychic heat before she could portal.

She wasn't getting up any time soon.

"Oh, I sent her back home. She's no longer necessary. Her only role was to get you and your team here. She is far too unpredictable in a battle. The wrong move can activate her portals and send her away, or worse, bring something terrible here. Now, let us speak," said the man.

Sylvester took a slow step forward. "Just to confirm, you are who I suspect? You are . . . Abel?"

"I am."

"Why are *you* here?"

"I'll explain."

He snapped his fingers and suddenly they were elsewhere. They were at what appeared to be a pool party at a Beverly Hills mansion — a real one, not a Hell version with blood for the water, for example.

Sylvester looked around. In the background, the Vogues began playing *Five O'clock World* and there were cheers from the pool party, which seemed grotesquely out of place in Hell. Yet, there it was, as if there were at a mansion in Beverly Hills. There were about fifty people scattered about, thirty women and twenty men, all in swimwear and all looking stunningly glamorous.

"The world . . . wasn't always this way," said Abel.

Then he snapped his fingers. They were suddenly in a large field of cotton. There was cotton as far as the eye could see. No planes, no machinery, no roads, no homes. It was oddly silent. The air was incredibly fresh.

"This was my world. In the beginning, the world was very simple. Back in the day, you know, we didn't have . . . layers. You wanted to talk to God, you talked to God. Now you need about fifty thousand lawyers and still have a wait of about a dozen centuries."

"I think that is exaggeration," said Sylvester with a half-smile.

Abel smiled. "A bit. Anyhow . . . Cain was mom and dad's first kid. I was the second. We did okay, got by. Cain was a farmer, and I was a shepherd, took care of the animals." He chuckled. "Don't ever get downwind of a goat with diarrhea, by the way."

"I'll remember that."

"God back in the day was what you call hands-on. You know, he hadn't put everything on autopilot like he has these days. Nowadays, he's like, you know, Stan Lee in the Marvel offices in 1972. But back then, we regularly made sacrifices. So, one day, I picked out the best sheep and brought him. Well, Cain tried to short-change God, keep the better fruit back for himself. Bad move. God was, like, way to go, Abel, and Cain got angry and jealous. Cain always had a temper. I mean, you're the first born in the world and you get grandiosity, I guess. Who wouldn't?"

"It would seem . . . inevitable."

"Yeah. So Cain lured me into the fields and pummeled me with a rock. God came back a bit later and asked Cain what happened, and Cain lied about it. God then ruined his crops. For good. Cain had a rough life after that."

There was a twinkle in Abel's eyes, and Sylvester frowned. "You seem . . . amused. As if there were a private joke."

"There was . . . for a time."

Sylvester's eyes widened. "Cain *didn't* lie. He didn't kill you."

Abel made a gun out of his hand and pointed it at Sylvester, fired, and blew away the fake smoke. "You got it, Immortal Man."

Shaking his head, Sylvester said, "I don't understand. How could God not know this — I can understand why he would ask Cain, to see Cain's response, but he must have known the truth."

"Oh, sure," said Abel, waving a hand. "He punished Cain for lying. Anyhow, I had punched out Cain first. He got pissy with me, and I slugged him, and he hit back, but just to get me off him. I landed and hit my head on a rock. Forensics in those days weren't what they are today, and no one had seen *Columbo*. Anyhow, that was it for me. Wham!"

"So, now . . . now . . . you are in Hell?"

"Yep. But that's not the big secret. The biggee is this — *I run this place*. Not Satan. I mean, give him a good book or some *Brady Bunch* reruns, and he sits on the couch and plays with himself and lets the place go to shit." He laughed. "I keep up the pretense. I mean, it's important. It's in the Bible and everything! I don't want to cause pandemonium," and he pointed up, "up there."

"How considerate," said Sylvester ruefully.

"Yeah. Care for a beer?"

Sylvester glared. "This is not a visitor's tour of the Christmas lights in St. Augustine, Abel. I am here on a mission."

"I know."

Sylvester paused. He now heard birds and the cotton plants blowing in the wind. "Are you here to *stop* me?"

"No," said Abel, and suddenly he looked serious. He looked a bit like Santa Claus, but now he looked like Santa about to deliver the blow to an eight-year-old kid that his crappy behavior had cost him Christmas.

"Are you here to *aid* me?"

"I know your *true* mission. It will affect Hell, affect me. After all this time . . . time you cannot comprehend, mortal man — despite your ridiculous moniker — time that is endless and never ending, which is not the same."

"Does that displease you?" asked Sylvester, rubbing his forehead. "I tire of the empty banter. *Speak your mind*!"

Abel suddenly turned into a rotting corpse and said, "I willingly give you your objective, your true objective, not the stated one. And for a simple reason. The gem that created Hell is now in Hitler's hand. Hitler is a conqueror. He already feels restrained by Hell. His objective is to use the gem to suck in Earth. It won't be Hell *on* Earth. It will be Earth *in* Hell."

Sylvester glared. "Madness."

"But possible. In fact, he's likely to win. The gem is that strong."

"I don't trust you."

"I figured as much. But I will aid you. In fact, I have been aiding you behind the scenes. I paid Hart and Taylor to get the team together and arrange the path for you to get here."

"Ah . . . aye, I see more clearly now," said Sylvester with a wry smile. "I take it you were behind the capsizing of the ferry on our initial entry as well?"

"Of course. I have the ability to rewrite the rules. But your team had to go through certain events to be prepared for this moment, and for things to be prepared for what comes after."

"Aye," said Sylvester, nodding grimly.

"Now come. Come with me. I will show you how to conquer Hitler . . . snotty old bastard . . . and achieve your . . . other goals."

Abel put a hand on Sylvester's back and laughed. "Come, let us go to the banks of the River Charon. On the way, we must prepare. Bravery and nobility can only take you so far. You will need firepower."

"Aye."

Chuckling, Abel added, "And fear not. We'll stay away from rocks."

Chapter Twelve
The Origin of Hell

"*You're* Tabitha's friend?" asked Nicole, completely surprised by the appearance of her new ally in hell, as well as the fact that she had appeared in what seemed to be a downtown office building in New York.

"Yup. I'm Fred. Fred Zarkowitzipzickh33, if you must know," said the penguin, flippers on its hips like a pissed off woman.

Nicole folded her arms over her naked chest. "You're a penguin."

"And you're a woman. So freakin' what? There's aliens here, too. Hell is equal opportunity, lady. Anyhow, if you want to redeem your butt and get outta here and help your friends, follow me," he said, turning and walking away, waving a flipper to encourage her to follow.

Nicole sighed. "I hate this place."

"We all do."

"Can I make some clothes here? I'm tired of running around naked."

"Yeah, and we're all tired of looking at your gross, flabby human form. Yeah, think up something. Make it quick," he said as they inexplicably exited the building and found themselves on the bank of the river Charon, the smell of blood overwhelming. "We gotta meet up with Meredith."

"Who is she?" asked Nicole, settling on an outfit that was purely cosmetic for comfort — black yoga pants, white sneakers, a red short-sleeved top with white stars on it, and a gold chain necklace.

Fred turned as they stood on the shore of human skin. "Nice outfit."

She glared at him. "Why are *you* running around naked? I'm tired of flippers and butts."

"I'm a penguin. We're always clothed in our feathers. Don't insult my flippers," he said, clearly offended.

"Sorry. Just joking."

He slapped his head. "This is Hell. Ya don't joke here."

"I do. Wait, there's a boat."

A small, four-seat boat approached. It was red and white with a small outboard motor, the type of boat Nicole had seen on many small lakes in summer. As it sped across the river of blood, screams came from the surface below where the blades cut those just under the surface. Nicole ignored it. She knew this place was not . . . normal. There was no way to cope with it, other than deny it.

In the boat were two people. One Nicole knew, for it was Dante, looking dapper. The other woman she didn't know.

The unknown woman looked to be about twenty-five years old. She had long, stringy blonde hair that looked dirty but wasn't, straight near the top but fading into long, wavy curls at about ear level, the hair extending between her shoulder blades, currently and usually held back by a black headband. Her nails were painted red, her lips maroon, her mascara blue and her light blush expertly applied. Her eyes were a dark blue, almost like the color of the deep ocean.

As Dante paused the boat's motor, the late Meredith Patience hopped out and waded through knee deep blood to the shore to shake Nicole's hand. "Hey, you're Nicole Smith. I've heard a lot about you."

"I don't know you from Adam," said Nicole, puzzled.

Dante approached and said, "This is Meredith Patience, a former Ops agent. She . . . killed many people in her quest for vengeance."

"Oh," said Nicole with obvious surprise. She remembered how the

Institute had always warned her Ops was violent . . . she was rapidly learning they weren't bullshitting her with that piece of information.

Nicole shook Meredith's hand.

"It's a little more complicated than that," said Fred.

Meredith looked at him. "Keep your beak shut, retard."

Dante interjected, "Enough banter. We must go. The final battle with Hitler is about to commence, and the destiny of both Hell and mankind stand in the balance. This is bigger than any event since Cain opened the doors."

"Bigger than the Super Bowl?" joked Nicole.

"Way so," said Meredith.

"I'm in," said Nicole, boarding the boat with Fred. "Uh, why is *he* coming?"

"He's actually quite skilled," said Meredith.

"At what? Annoying people?" asked Nicole.

Meredith laughed as she got into the boat. The boat had four seats, two each facing the other. Charon manned the directional post and ignored them. Nicole sat with Meredith to her right. Across from Nicole sat Fred, and to his left sat Dante.

"Aw, give him a break, Nicole. Fred's one of the oldest guys here."

Nicole gave them both a look. "I find that hard to buy."

"That's 'cause you don't know shit, Smith."

Meredith looked at Fred. "You might as well tell her."

"Tell me what?" asked Nicole, rolling her eyes. "This back-and-forth banter is annoying enough among women, but between women and penguin, it's too much. Let's get serious." She pointed at Dante. "He seems pretty fucking serious, and I'm sure the destiny of mankind is something we should be discussing."

"Agreed," said Meredith. She looked at Fred. "You have the best knowledge of this place. Lay it on her."

Fred took a deep breath, rubbed a flipper over his forehead, and started talking. "Sure, Patience. Okay . . . Smith, you ever read the Bible?"

"Everyone has. I would not say I am a devout Christian . . . I am familiar with the concepts, but I'm more of a . . . holist. I believe all life is connected, and the life force, our aura, unites us. I do believe in God. I just don't believe in tradition and ritual."

"Okay. Long-winded fuckin' answer, but I can work with it," said Fred. "Back in the beginning, God created Adam and Eve."

"Right."

"Wrong!" he shouted, kicking her left shin with his right foot.

"Hey!" she shouted. "That hurt."

"Stop being an emo baby. The fact is, mankind and Earth . . . in the scheme just of our galaxy, let alone the universe, is very young. God was busy making all sorts of alien shit long before he came up with the idea of Earth. He created several alien galaxies, a few of which developed the idea of space-travel and arrived on Earth via tachyonic anti-matter warp drive."

Meredith interjected, "Nicole isn't part of Ops, so she may not be familiar with portal gems and their creation."

"Then fuck her, she can take a science class when she gets her flabby human, tit-sucking ass outta here."

Nicole said, "I'll catch up. Go on."

"Anyhow, the point is, one of those aliens landed on Earth and crashed. The gem infused Earth with enough improbability matrix to kick off life. This was never God's plan. He was busy mowing the yard or something off in Alpha Centuri, but when he got his ass around to looking back at Earth, he saw what was up and thought it might be fun. After all, God is an artist at heart. So he decided to make Earth into a new planet, the only planet in this solar system with life, and see what would happen. When you're omnipotent and immortal, curiosity is all that runs your life."

Nicole glanced at Meredith. "Is this for real?"

"Yeah . . . it's on good authority. Imagine this oratory narrated by John Facenda or James Earl Jones and it goes down better."

Fred cleared his throat. "Anyyyyyyyyyyyy how, if I may continue," and Nicole waved a hand, so he did, "God created Adam and Eve. He had his little monkeys. He showed them the garden, gave them some birds and the bees basics, and then," and he held up a flipper, "he gave them the gem. Then he went back to dealing with some alien races, because frankly he was much more interested in them than his little monkeys."

"Why leave the gem?" asked Nicole, still trying to grasp that she was getting the basics of humanity from a foul-mouthed penguin while riding on a boat in a river of blood in Hell. This wasn't quite how she had pictured Ops.

"Basically, in case they found they needed anything he hadn't thought of. I mean, the guy had a lot on his mind, floating around form galaxy to galaxy. He didn't have the time to micro-manage.

"The gem was incredibly powerful, thousands of times more powerful than a typical gem. It was basically a magic lamp with a genie. Anything they wanted, they could have. All that stuff about the garden is mostly allegory."

"I know the man who wrote Genesis," said Dante with a smile. "I met him on one of my trips to Heaven."

"You went to Heaven?" asked Meredith with surprise.

"I get around. I document *all*," said Dante.

"Anyyyyyyyyyyyy-how, as I was saying, they had the gem. But they found God had done a kick-ass job, and they didn't need shit. They got busy having babies, doing the garden up, you know how it is when you have kids.

"Things were fine. Cain was born. First monkey baby in the world."

"Hey, lay off the monkey stuff," said Nicole.

"Whatever. The problem was, God made Adam and Eve . . . that rib stuff is all allegory . . . but thereafter, all humans were made conventionally — and rather amazingly, without internet porn as inspiration." Nicole rolled her eyes and Fred continued. "Cain has an interesting story, but we can get into that later, assuming we stop Hitler. Anyhow, with normal human birth came normal human drives. God wanted to see if man could rise to his level. Didn't quite work."

"Cain killed his brother Abel, right?" asked Nicole.

"Sort of. And that's where the gem comes in. Cain realized the gem could allow them to have anything, so why strive when he could have it anyhow? But by the time Cain figured this out, Adam had put

Abel in charge of the gem, already realizing Cain was a bit of a . . . well, black sheep, shall we say. No offense to the ovine."

"I'm sure they aren't offended," said Dante.

"I'm sure they are. Fucking sheep can be real ass-kickers, but they can't hear me here," said Fred. He then spit over the side and said, "Anyhow, a fight broke out. Abel attacked Cain, which is something the Bible missed. The net result was that Cain killed Abel by accident, and immediately had a massive case of conscience and the guilts like nobody's business. And that's where the problems started."

"Because he regretted it?" asked Nicole, obviously confused.

"Yep. Because he also had the gem. The gem was huge, incredibly powerful. Because of that, it drew on the subconscious of those around it, which at the time was only Cain 'cause Abel was dead. Cain's regret was profound, and he sought redemption. That came via his subconscious and the creation of Hell."

"I'm not exactly a biblical scholar, but I thought God created Hell to imprison Satan," said Meredith.

Fred shook his head. "Popular myth. Yeah, Satan got his ass stuck down here, but by that point, Hell was *already here*. Like any blank slate dimension, once it is created, it has a life of its own. The key is the power of this gem. It's *thousands* of times more powerful than a typical portal gem. Once it drew on Cain's subconscious, it simply continued to feed on those who felt they deserved to be here and, WHOOOOP, it sucks them in," he said, clapping his flippers.

"Who thinks they deserve to be here?" asked Nicole incredulously.

Fred pointed a flipper at his head. "Ya'd be surprised."

Dante said, "Man's conscience condemns him, but the gem holds man fast in Hell. Some escape. Not many. Not all deserve to. Like this one." He pointed at Fred.

"What did you do? Steal some fish?" asked Meredith.

Fred chuckled. "I was the first penguin serial killer. I liked killing other penguins. They cast me out and I froze to death." He shook his head. "I didn't think the whole killer thing through."

Nicole said, "I could care less. How do souls get out?"

"God gets some people out, those with strong belief systems, those not beaten down by Hell. Otherwise, well, if you get a gem, you can portal out. That's not easy. Hell is somewhat bureaucratic. It's divided into regions, but more complicated now than when Dante was first here. There's mostly a few plyers in charge of everything, and they gather up anything paranormal. So, to assemble the power to get out is hard, and often that means help from rituals on Earth."

"Which is why we're finding Hitler," said Meredith, her eyes narrowing. "He's become the dominant paranormal collector in Hell, and he was strong to start with. He's gathered enough now to make his move and take over Hell, including the gem."

Before Nicole could ask for clarification, they pulled to a dock made of human bone that linked to an island made of a whale's skeleton. But the whale had eyes and screamed from time to time.

"Last stop, gals," said Fred, and he and Dante assisted them off the boat.

"Thanks. You're pretty polite for a serial killer," said Nicole.

"Ah, you know, you grow out of things after a few thousand years in Hell. Up this way. We gotta meet a guy."

They walked and Nicole saw a man waving at them — Sylvester.

Meredith ran forward and hugged him. "My God, it *is* you. They said you were part of this, but I wasn't sure."

They broke the embrace, and he shook his head. "We're here to stop the Horal. How are you here? You cannot be here."

Meredith smiled. "I'm not here . . . I mean, I wasn't sent here when I . . . you know," and she made a throat slashing gesture. "I'm here . . . it's complicated."

"Well, we got a few minutes. We gotta walk up the trail of bile to get to our last partner," said Fred.

Dante said, "I've come far enough with you, Miss Meredith Patience. I must relocate to prepare to chronicle the final battle for Hell. I wish you success on your endeavor."

"Thanks for the help, Danny boy."

Dante shook all their hands and said, "I will write another fine tale about you."

Once he was out of earshot, Fred said, "Egotistical jerk. C'mon, follow me."

They started walking up a trail of yellow bile that smelled awful, walking through a forest of arms and fingers that had mutated into trees and leaves. It was grotesque, but none of them paid attention. They knew denial was their only defense.

Sylvester looked at Meredith. "I'm so sorry for how everything ended."

"It's over, water under the bile, so to speak," she said, but she looked sad. "What is Sam's status?"

Sylvester stared hard at her. "You seem to know a great deal of our situation."

She gave him a half-smile. "You'd be surprised."

Sylvester said, "Sam is still in a coma. He sent us here to destroy something called the Horal, the aliens that gave us Quotient. I'm surprised you didn't know that. Did you not come from Heaven?"

"Not so much, I don't know about any of that. See . . . well," and she took a deep breath, "when I died, I was sort of . . . stuck . . . in limbo. I wasn't sure if I was going up or down. I killed a lot of people and what I did to Necra was . . . wrong on every level. But I was consumed by PTSD, by the urge to act out revenge against Zenith on the only TM around. It was wrong. It wasn't an excuse. But it was a factor. So, I didn't feel like I was Ted Bundy or something. But I was . . . confused. Mentally ill."

"Reasonable," said Sylvester.

"I guess. You're always so confident."

He snorted. "Hardly. Please, continue."

"There are many others in limbo. It takes time to adjust to death, especially when it's instant and violent. Some people stay there years, even decades, even a few people there for centuries. One of them . . . one of them . . . was Zenith."

She closed her eyes and stopped walking. Nicole put a hand on her, and Sylvester said, "A shock, I imagine."

"Yesssssssssss," she hissed. "God, the hate I felt for that woman."

Sylvester nodded. Being in charge of Ops, he was well aware of the flashback Meredith unearthed while torturing Necra to death in Africa in 2017. While Zenith's captive in 2014, Meredith was forced to drink the liquified remains of a guard she had replaced and Zenith had subsequently killed.

Nicole was not aware of this memory, of course. Nor did she ask. The look of hate on Meredith's face scared her . . . scared her while she was in Hell walking on bile. It was that fucking scary.

"But she . . . was a broken woman, an old woman . . . and I . . . I wanted to kill her even though we were both dead, if that makes sense. But she told me . . . Beth's soul could be reconstructed."

"Beth?" asked Nicole.

Fred said, "Her sister was Zenith's soul-slave and when Zenith was losing, she destroyed it."

Now Nicole stopped walking. "My God, that's horrible."

Fred shrugged. "I've heard worse."

They resumed walking and Meredith said to Nicole, "I don't know if you know anything about me. I guess not. But when I was a teenager, Zenith murdered my mother and father and made Beth a zombie soul-slave. I fought for years to free her, and instead got captured and enslaved. They used me like a robot to help this drilling project and punished me by liquefying a corpse and . . . making me drink it."

Nicole was stunned. "I . . . don't know what to say. I'm sorry. That's horrific."

"Well . . . don't worry about it. Sam helped me heal." She paused. "Uh, full disclosure. I was working with Tabitha to get you here as well. I just . . . I knew it was important. I have no idea why or what Tabitha wanted, but she really helped out."

Nicole's eyes narrowed. She wasn't sure if Meredith was bullshitting her or not, but it didn't seem like she was. Nicole merely said, "Tabitha and I had . . . issues to resolve. It's okay."

"Good, good. Anyhow, I was killed in May of 202 by Calico Kelkirk in a battle on Storm Island . . . what year did you come down here, anyhow?"

"Oh, '21."

"Oh. Not so long then. Uh, anyhow, let's see . . . well, so Zenith in limbo. She told me Beth's soul could be reconstructed, but only using a massive amount of power. The power of the gem used to generate Hell."

"Oh," said Nicole.

Sylvester was more concerned. "You seek to wrench the gem from Hell and save Beth? Would not that disrupt the entire blank dimension of Hell."

"I can't do it that way. I just need proximity."

"Based on what Zenith said?" asked Sylvester skeptically.

Meredith shook her head. "No. Zenith had others there, and they all agreed. So . . . I sent myself here. Not right away. They said to wait, because they knew from time-to-time living entities pass into Hell. When this team popped through, I had my chance. I knew it was an Ops team, but I didn't know any of the members."

"It's good you're here. We are in the end-game," said Sylvester grimly.

"What does that flippin' mean?" asked Fred.

"I have the same question, but with better English," said Nicole.

Sylvester said, "I have learned from a source that Hitler has obtained the gem . . . and he plans to use it to suck in all of Earth. It won't be Hell on Earth. It will be Earth in Hell."

"You've gotta be kidding," said Nicole.

Sylvester shook his head. "No. Dead serious. The problem is that this won't work, due to the nature of the gem. He'll wind up creating a blank slate dimension that merges Earth and Hell and will be totally out of his control."

"So, it will be Hell without rules?" asked Meredith.

"Yep."

"Sounds like Black Friday," muttered Nicole. "How do we stop him?"

"We find our other friends . . . and we prepare for battle. You see, I need the gem myself, to stop the Horal."

"After I use it to restore Beth," said Meredith tersely.

"Of course, my dear. But neither of us can achieve our end-game without obtaining the gem, meaning we must stop Hitler. Come. We must portal to the volcanic lands of the Ninth Circle where Hitler now makes his home."

Chapter Thirteen
World War II Part II

"Whoa," was all anyone said, and this was said by Nicole.

They stood staring, arriving on a rocky hillside that looked like it was thousands of different rocks from all over the world thrown together. It was that and more, as it included the skulls of citizens of Hell, crying as they were crushed under the weight repeatedly throughout time.

The sky was red and full of smoke, and all around them were hilltops with lava. The result was an atmosphere that was incredibly loud, incredibly hot, very brightly lit, and shaded red.

Around the rims of the volcanoes were thousands of torture victims. Some were on inverted crosses, some on poles, some being spit roasted, some in pieces, but all were screaming and crying as their anguish and torture was used to feed their owner.

Hitler.

He stood on the crown of the hillside in full, gray uniform with the red Nazi emblem, standing next to a small pool table with two chairs that were made of bone and cartilage. It had an umbrella of an alien's skin, the skin sentient and whining in some alien, obscure language.

In Hitler's right hand he held a small, emerald gem that was about the size of a baseball. In gem terms, that made it huge. Most gems were the size of a pencil eraser, perhaps as big as a fingernail. In his left hand, he held a riding crop.

Suddenly, Sylvester saw a rip in space to their left. Through it stepped Tripper and Geneva.

"My friends!"

"Sylvester! *Meredith*! Nicole!" said Geneva, and she hugged Sylvester. "It's good to see you, to see you all. My God, Meredith, how are you here? What's going on?"

"This is the end-game," said Sylvester.

"I'm here from Limbo, here to help," said Meredith quickly.

"Yeah, reckon I'm a gonna guess this is the place for the showdown," said Tripper nervously, shaking Nicole's hand.

Sylvester asked, "Where did you come from?"

"Hitler's castle," said Tripper, not taking his eyes off Hitler. Of all the things in the world or out of it that Tripper despised, Hitler was at the top of the list. In fact, he was on a list of his own.

"Anyone else with you?" asked Sylvester.

Geneva looked sad, "No. We were five — we found Tripper's old friend, Krissy, and Little Jack's siters. We were separated. Only Tripper and I made it here. Krissy lost herself to her . . . weaknesses. And apparently, Little Jack's sisters are redeemed and back on Earth."

"Aye, that 'tis good news for the sisters. As for Krissy, most fall in Hell. Had they strength of character, they would not be in Hell to being with," said Sylvester. "This is our team."

Geneva shouted to be heard. "Against Hitler? Uh, not to sound defeatist, Sylvester, but Hitler looks pretty confident."

"Evil always does," said Sylvester.

Geneva snapped her fingers. "Well, he's in for a surprise, because I can channel here. Tripper?"

"Yep."

Nicole and Meredith nodded as well.

Sylvester said, "We must be in localized space where your auras are stronger . . . perhaps we are close to a rupture that leads to Earth or some other plain."

Nicole pointed and said, "Something's coming over the ridge."

She was right. To Hitler's left came Cerberus, the three-headed dog that was the guardian of Hell. This incarnation of Cerberus looked like a pit-bull with three heads of pit-bull shape and glowing red eyes. He had a spiked collar and was the size of a semi-truck and trailer.

"Man, I ain't gonna scoop up his crap," said Tripper nervously.

On the other side was a huge man about seven-six and a solid, bulky 400 pounds who strode naked. He had a thick brow and long, black hair. His look was one of the Devil himself. This was Vlad the Impaler, his looks greatly improved by a few centuries in Hell.

"Who's he?" asked Nicole.

Geneva was a very intelligent, well-read woman. But even she wasn't certain. "I don't know."

Sylvester grimly said, "I know. He has changed in Hell, but that is undoubtedly Vlad the Impaler."

"Y'all sure?" asked Tripper.

"Yes." He looked at Tripper. "There's a certain . . . aural sense . . . even in Hell . . . that those of us cursed share . . . it is he." He grunted. "Perhaps this is why we can channel. The aural blockers are lifted so these creatures can destroy us. They are channelers as well."

"Go back. Cerberus was cursed?" asked Geneva with surprise.

"There's much to him, but suffice it to say, he is not here to exchange Christmas cards with us," said Sylvester grimly.

Meredith had been unusually quiet, just staring at the gem. Finally, she said, "I don't give a flying fuck about anything except getting that gem."

Suddenly, a man appeared. He was a handsome man with curly brown hair, light blue eyes, a masculine jaw, and a well-built body. He looked a little like a forty-year-old Dan Marino.

"Dante?" said Geneva, surprised by his sudden appearance, recognizing him from her first trip to Hell. "What are you doing here?"

He held up the book. "I have come to chronicle. This is the most important battle in the history of mankind. This is the battle that will either be the final battle in Hell, or lock Hell and Earth in an eternal, endless struggle."

"So no pressure then," said Nicole.

"We won't fuck this up," snapped Meredith.

Geneva studied Dante. "Are you serious or just being melodramatic to pump up sales?"

Dante laughed. "I chronicle, Miss Kane. It is both my reward for my first visit . . . and my own curse."

Geneva gave him a sardonic look. "Yeah, I know that feeling."

"Guys, while you're shooting the shit, the army of evil bastards from Hell is advancing," said Nicole nervously. "I vote retreat."

Meredith slammed a fit into her palm. "Fuck no. I'm getting that gem if I gotta fight through every fucking maggot-fuck in this place."

"We need a plan," snapped Geneva. She didn't ask why Meredith wanted the gem. She could guess its value to her, and wasn't about to oppose her, anyways.

Tripper said, "Meredith's right. If Hitler has the gem, it's the key. Forget everyone else. Let's create a wedge to get to him and separate him from the gem. That's priority."

Dante nodded like the fan of a football team that always screws it up in the end. He knew this wouldn't work.

And it didn't.

The first problem was that Sylvester ran away immediately.

"Uh, our leader just ran," said Nicole, looking around nervously. It was very loud now, the roar of their enemies, the barking of Cerberus, and the continual eruptions all combining into one seemingly endless rumble.

"He must have a plan, so let him get to it," said Geneva immediately. And she was confident she was correct. "We must advance. I'll take the point."

"We just gonna go right up the volcano at him?"

"I don't see any other way," said Geneva.

Tripper glared upwards at the man he hated above all others, more than Trout, more than the men that raped and killed Caroline, more than the doctor that was useless when his brother died of the flu. "Works for me."

Nicole glanced at Meredith as Cerberus led the advance down the volcano. "This is why I'm a cat and not a dog person."

Dante suddenly rose and hovered in a cross-legged position about twenty yards above the combat zone. He had a journal and an old-fashioned, yellow, number two lead pencil. He'd bitten off the eraser.

He began his chronicle.

Immediately, it was clear Geneva's powers were exponentially stronger than at any point in her life. After battling Calico Kelkirk in Germany and being attacked with a tachyon surge, Geneva had gained probability powers that were baffling. She was able to actually change the structure of objects, but it was beyond her control. She'd only been experimenting with this ability for a couple of months, but being in Hell, she was constrained only by her mental capabilities, and those were among the most formidable of anyone living.

Geneva began storming the hill, turning those around her into glass.

Nicole gasped and looked at Meredith. "She can do that?"

"That's news to me. Forget it, we can flank Hitler to the side."

Tripper watched, a bit in awe as Geneva stormed up the hill, turning everything to glass. Demons, aliens, animals, humans, all turned to glass when they got within fifty feet of her. They broke and cracked as they were urn into by others, their shards of their souls mixing together in the volcanic rock. They weren't dead or destroyed, but they would need decades to reassemble their . . . pieces.

"Well . . . gol'darn," he muttered to himself.

But as the team closed in on Hitler, it got tougher. He had a shield immediately around him. He rose with a pompous look on his face. He moved to a clearing at the rim of the volcano, the opening behind him, so he couldn't be taken by a rear advance.

"Come, Tripper. Come be todt, as you long deserve!"

Tripper said nothing. He was to Hitler's far right, Geneva next, then Nicole, then Meredith.

Cerberus was the last one standing. He sat at Hitler's side and snarled.

"Your pet dog won't help you," said Meredith.

She charged him.

Cerberus didn't move. But Hitler did. He grabbed the aural energy Geneva had been using to turn everyone to glass and snatched it telekinetically as if he were a person physically grabbing ribbon. Then he hurled it back at the team.

They screamed.

And they were turned to glass, except for Geneva, who was only very slowly turning. She fell to her hands and knees, half glass, half human, screaming as her insides were ripped up.

"Now we end this game!" shouted Hitler.

Cerberus barked and wagged his tail.

Geneva collapsed.

Chapter Fourteen
Taking Control

"No . . . no . . . get . . . up," gasped Geneva Kane, hitting herself in the side, trying to force herself to her feet, her body now mostly glass.

But she couldn't do it.

Hitler stepped forward and stepped hard on her hand, jamming it between his boots and the lava rock, cracking fingers. Geneva felt the pain but didn't scream. Her entire body was ravaged by pain, as if her blood had turned to glass as well, slowing slicing itself up from the inside.

"Ach, you are most determined. It matters not. Your others . . . are dispatched."

Cerberus laughed and barked.

Slowly, Geneva raised her head. She knew she was dying . . . no, that wasn't right. She was in Hell. She was . . . dissipating? Was her soul being destroyed?

She looked around and saw the entire team had been turned into glass.

Hitler giggled maniacally. His eyes were uneven in his head, and she knew he was insane — even by the standards of Hell. "I sell to highest bidder. You . . . will soon be glass as well."

Geneva screamed in agony and terror. She knew he was right. Her body was changing . . . she was horrified, so horrified she thought she might lose her mind, because in Hell one wasn't granted the relief of losing consciousness from pain — be it mental or physical.

Hitler grabbed her hair and started dragging her across the rock. She couldn't fight back. As he dragged her, pieces of her glass fingers and toes broke off and he said, "You were a fool. You were on a fool's errand from the start. You will live out your life as a statue in my castle."

"No."

Hitler stopped, and stunned Geneva turned her head — a difficult chore at this point — and they saw Sylvester standing at the top of the ridge.

Before Hitler could respond, thousands . . . perhaps *hundreds of thousands* of . . . people . . . were surrounding them. They were all nude, but all armed with some type of gun.

Startled, Hitler let go of Geneva's hair and fell back. As soon as he let go, she felt something change. She felt power. Desperately, she focused on it, as if she were channeling — perhaps she was, but instead of channeling an element, she was just channeling thought itself, to reshape her body. She could feel herself turning, if not human, at least less like . . . glass.

Sylvester stood above them all on the back of some type of gigantic woolly mammoth that had red eyes and tusks at least ten yards long. He blew a trumpet made of bone. Nude, he pointed at Hitler and shouted, "Your reign is over. *I am the master of Hell now.* I am the ruler here . . . and you will be dispatched from the Ninth Circle!"

"Nein! Nein!"

Geneva saw his fear and felt a rush of joy. She suddenly was herself again, and she lunged at Hitler, hitting him in the right knee with such force that she dislocated it.

Cerberus turned tall and ran.

He screamed, but she ignored it, rolling and pulling him with her down a hill of ash towards molten lava below. She knew it would hurt, but that she could survive it. She hoped he *couldn't*, for she desperately wished to put an end to him once and for all.

"Take them all, but save the glass figures!" shouted Sylvester, but even as he said this, the others started to change back into human form.

The thousands of troops moved forward like ants overrunning a corpse in the Amazon.

Hitler said, "Nein . . . nein!"

Geneva moved to take him, but he suddenly realized the danger. He dodged a channeling attempt, Geneva using wind and earth control to send lava at him. This required much less effort than her probability channeling, especially as lava was simply earth in molten form. Hitler turned and ran towards an odd pier at the bottom of a lake of bubbling fat, heads bobbing in the lake trying not to drown.

"Tripper!" shouted Geneva, pointing at Hitler.

"C'mon!"

At the pier were boats, except they weren't boats. They were something like giant flying owls without feathers, just pink skin. There were five, chained to the pier by tendrils. They were talking like old women at a Bingo match.

"Hey," shouted one of them as Hitler jumped on its back and grabbed horse reigns that were hooked around its neck.

"Fly, dolt!" shouted Hitler.

The owl took off flying as Hitler cut the lines tethering it to the dock.

Tripper and Geneva tried to channel wind, but the owl, which was the size of a small Cesena, banked upwards.

"We gotta follow! Get aboard!" shouted Tripper, pointing at the owls.

Geneva jumped on her owl. "Uh, giddyap!"

"I'm not a fucking cowboy, bitch. But I'll go get that fuck. I hate Hitler. He owes me money," snapped her owl.

Geneva snapped the tendril tie, and they were airborne.

Tripper jumped on his owl and said, "Well, y'all got any comments?"

"I hate niggers, and I hate women, and I hate this place. Get me outta here and I'll eat Hitler for lunch."

"Deal."

And then they were off.

The owls flew like owls, but they had no feathers, just wings of bone and skin. In essence, Tripper realized quickly, this was more like flying a plane. He just had to bank the owl's head up and down to get it to move.

Geneva realized this a well, and they started closing in on Hitler, who had to bank back down towards a desert plain because one of the several volcanos in the area erupted.

"We got 'im now, lady!" shouted Geneva's owl.

"Geneva!"

"Zack! Man, I've been waiting *decades* to collect! I gave him a ride to the fourth level once and he stiffed my tip."

"Uh, not to offend, but I have no money."

"No worries. I like you."

Geneva said nervously, "Well, good. I like you, too. Uh, he's dropping."

"Trying to shake us, loser fuck! Hold tight. If you fall off, I'm not coming back."

Geneva held on to the owl's neck like a little girl holding onto a roller coaster being ridden for the first time and said, "Give it all you've got."

Tripper's owl said, "Me and Zack over there can pincer him."

"Do it and talk less. I'm O'Sullivan, by the by."

"Zimbo."

"Zimbo?"

"Yeah, it's a long story. Hold tight."

Hitler turned and saw Geneva closing in on the right, Tripper on the left. Cursing, he kicked into the side of his owl and said, "Schnell! Schnell! Cursed creature!"

"Hey, I don't have to take this shit," said Hitler's owl suddenly, and it bucked and flipped him off.

Hitler screamed.

Zimbo made a dive for him, and Hitler landed on his back.

Tripper was suddenly face to face with the most hated paranormal in the history of the world once again, and ready to battle and defeat him once again. Tripper's one true act of bravery was battling Hitler. It was the one battle he had no fear of losing.

He quickly raised his cane like a club and slammed it towards Hitler's head, but Hitler blocked it with his left forearm.

"Wretched American!"

"Proud of it, scum-bag!" shouted Tripper, trying to move and trip Hitler. He was also trying to blow Hitler into the desert below, but that was impossible. Zimbo was keeping his flight level to slowly descend and land in the desert.

"Y'all is done for good this time," shouted Tripper, raising his cane like a club.

Hitler had hold of the reigns and had good footing. Tripper didn't. Hitler drove the heel of his boot into Zimbo, hoping to cause him to jerk and shake Tripper off.

"Jerk!" shouted Zimbo suddenly, and he came to a dead stop.

Tripper flew forward and crashed into Hitler, adroitly moving his cane in front. The cane landed on Hitler's neck and pinned him to Zimbo's back.

Zimbo started to drop.

Tripper shouted, "Y'all is finished! I'll crush your soul!"

Zimbo wasn't that far above the ground, and they were over the desert sand, which was actually the faces of the denizens of Hell. There was massive wailing as Zimbo dropped . . . and he landed hard.

The impact thrust Tripper's cane down, and he snapped Hitler's neck.

Tripper lay on the body for a moment, staring at the dead eyes, a little shocked he'd actually won. He wasn't sure how Hitler was dead. This was Hell. Was this Hitler's Hell, losing to Tripper? Then he remembered the gem. He fished it out of Hitler's pocket.

"Zimbo, I owe y'all a beer."

"Don't worry about it. Guy has always been a fucking pain. He won't stay out long, though. Obviously, death isn't permanent in Hell. Think about a mystical cage."

"Okay," he said, wondering why he was listening to a talking, giant, flying owl-like creature. Then again, why was he here? He focused and made a metal cage.

"Perfect. Throw his ass in. As long as you're here, the mental energy will hold him."

"And when I go back?"

Zimbo shrugged. "That's up to whoever winds up in charge after this mess. Better check on your friends."

"Right. Thanks."

"Don't forget the beer."

Tripper concentrated and whistled up four kegs of beer. "Have fun."

Zimbo shot out his tongue like a pitchfork. It penetrated the keg, and he began sucking down.

Tripper approached Geneva, who was racing to his side. She threw her arms around him and said, "I can't believe you did that."

"It weren't nothin'."

She just shook her head and they quickly walked to a clearing at the very top of the volcano where Sylvester, Meredith, and Nicole stood near Sylvester's woolly mammoth creature.

"What's going on? You look like we're partying at the beach," said Geneva with alarm. The volcano erupted continuously, but there was no lava.

"Just waiting," said Sylvester grimly.

"For what?" asked Geneva, wiping her hair out of her face.

Sylvester took the gem from Tripper, carefully eyed by Meredith. Then Sylvester nodded. "Yes, I can feel the power now. I should shortly hear the signal."

At that moment, in his coma again, even if just for a minute, Sam Grant stood up and stretched.

Normally, Sam Grant was slightly balding, his brown, curly hair fading to gray. He had brown eyes and a short, five-foot and eight-inch wiry frame. He also had a big nose that looked a bit like a vulture's beak. Born and raised in Racine, he had left the Midwest behind, but it was still inside him. But now, he looked like a battle-weary Viking. He had a very long and full beard, mustache, and had gotten very fat. And old. Sam had just turned fifty-two, but he looked closer to seventy. He had been in a coma since Ops defeated Quotient in January. Hell time didn't necessarily correlate to Earth time. Only moments had passed on Earth to this point.

"Sam, it's the eighth inning. You're late for that seventh inning stretch thing," said his blonde late wife, Bam, clearly bored. A few drops of rain began to fall on the small, semi-pro baseball field.

Then Sam began to laugh hysterically and threw his arms wide.

Rain began to fall. The players and fans scurried for cover, but not Sam. He merely stood there laughing, face up and taking in the rain.

Meredith, who like Bam was purely a creation of Sam's subconscious, looked at Bam. "What do we do?"

Bam said, "I'll handle it."

Meredith ducked under the bleachers, out of the downpour.

Bam held her husband's left arm and said, "Sam, you're acting nuts."

Then Quotient appeared over the field, his yellowish blob-self glaring with the single eye, and about twenty feet in diameter, larger than normal.

"Oh, God," said Bam. "I'm scared."

"Be calm. It's not Quotient, dear. It's Jagroth," he said, referring to the Horal that had helped through the process of the battle with Quotient and subsequent coma.[5]

Jagorth's thoughts were in their head. "It is accomplished, SamGrant. Your actions were wise."

Then Jagroth vanished.

The rain stopped.

Sam turned to Bam. "This entire mission, it was never about stopping the Horal, Bam. *Never.* The Horal *can't* be stopped any more than electricity or solar flares or volcanos. They are part of the nature of reality."

---

[5] See TM 4.0 "Merger"

"Then . . . what *was* it about?"

"*Destroying Hell*?" asked Geneva, her mouth literally dropping with astonishment at Sylvester's proclamation.

"Yes."

"But . . . but . . . I don't understand," said Geneva.

Sylvester smiled gently. "When Sam held the power of the Horal in his mind, during the merger created by Mary Richardson and Jennifer Saunders, he was able to clearly see what the Horal are. *They are merely the beings that make up existence. They are living quantum physics.* Observing them is dangerous, it changes their nature. They aren't gods, but they have nearly omnipotent power. We are less than ants to them. But in seeing this, Sam realized he could leech some of their power and accomplish the one mission that seemed beyond the task of Ops."

"Quantum physics?" said Nicole, looking like she just flunked the SAT.

Geneva turned to her and said, "Quickly and simply: The act of observation is critical in quantum physics. Early in the field, scientists were baffled to find that simply observing an experiment influenced the outcome. For example, an electron acted like a wave when not observed, but the act of observing it caused the wave to collapse and the electron to behave instead like a particle. Scientists now appreciate that the term "observation" is misleading, suggesting that consciousness is involved. Instead, "measurement" better describes the effect, in which a change in outcome may be caused by the interaction between the quantum phenomenon and the external environment, including the device used to measure the phenomenon."

Nicole and Meredith both looked bewildered. Nicole finally said, "I hope they pay you a lot, because you sure are smart."

Ignoring her, Geneva turned with wide eyes to Sylvester. "Wait. Wait. The Horal . . . the mission!"

"You and Sam frequently discussed it, how to free all the people here."

"Destroying Hell," said Geneva, nodding, starting to understand. "I've craved that since I was falsely held here. No one deserves this."

"Agreed. Sam found a way, aided by Jagroth of the Horal . . . but to do it, he had to establish his own leader here and give you a mission that was pure of heart. *He knew you could never defeat Hell if you sought to defeat Hell.* Human psychology simply doesn't work that way. You had to be on a mission to imprison someone or something in Hell, which became the Horal."

"Wait, Sylvester," said Meredith slowly. "Where does the gem fit in?"

Sylvester threw it up in the air and caught it like a baseball. "Ah, 'tis is a basic case of the cart before the horse. It does no good to destroy Hell if it can be recreated. It was necessary to secure the gem prior to starting the deconstruction."

"Did he . . . did he know it would help me save Beth?"

"I do not know. It's possible."

Geneva put her hands on her hips, suddenly in awe. "Sam figured all of this out?"

"He had help, of course. As I said, one of the Horal, Jagroth, aided him to help make up for the mess created by Quotient — and Horus in the world of the Outcasts. Not all of the Horal were agreed on this. Another reason for the covert operation. Sam in a coma was considered harmless."

Tripper suddenly laughed and slapped his knees. "Reckon that damn ol' turkey-fucker Grant is trickier than any of us! I may have well underestimated that boy."

"I'm sure he'll forgive you," said Geneva dryly.

"There is a caveat," said Sylvester suddenly.

"I knew there was a catch. There always is," said Meredith.

"I . . . I will remain. I will be leading the . . . redistribution of Hell."

Everyone was stunned. Meredith finally spat out, "You gotta be kidding!"

"It was always part of the plan." He smiled. "I sensed it even before we left. Sam knew I was the man for this job. And fear not. There are billions here in Hell. We must find the proper path for all of them. Hell is finished. No one new will come here, unless they escape prematurely and are portaled back — it will take decades to place everyone here in their proper place."

"Good Lord," said Nicole, and it was immediately obvious to all of them that things had changed, because she wasn't struck by pain.

Tripper suddenly pointed his cane at Sylvester. "Reckon there ain't no proper place for Hitler and his like."

"You'd be surprised. They all have a role to play. Putting them in their proper place, my friend, does not mean they go back to Earth and resume their roles. Hell hath ended. But there will still be a . . . retaining dimension." He chuckled. "Perhaps a planet with nothing but monks chanting or ostriches that sing."

Tripper laughed. "Y'all is devious, old man."

"Perhaps."

"Well, you're gonna need to do a lot of rebranding," said Nicole, trying to make a joke. Everyone ignored her.

Geneva stepped forward. "Sylvester, you're the man for the job."

"I will have Jagroth's aid for a time, to ensure stability. But I appreciate your confidence."

"Will we ever see you again?" she asked, tears in her eyes.

"Of this I am most certain, that there is no way to predict the unpredictable. I aim to do so." He smiled. "So, take care of yourself and make sure you live a long life!"

She smiled. "Then I'll take that as a yes, and I will make that promise."

"Now, not to be a rude host, but you must all leave. You have your roles to fulfill, and the rewrite cannot commence until all living are out of here — some of you to Heaven, and Tripper, you, Geneva and Nicole must go back to mundane life."

Meredith said, "But I need the gem to restore Beth!"

"No, you don't."

Stunned, Meredith turned to see her sister, Beth, in the pure form of her soul, a mix of yellow and purple light. She spoke via telepathy and said, "I will see you in Heaven shortly."

Then she was gone.

Meredith just said, "Whoa."

Geneva hugged her. "I'm pleased for you, my friend."

"Thanks."

Turning to Sylvester, she said with distress, "Our memories of you will fade."

"Jagroth can allow you to retain memory of this visit."

"I appreciate that," said Geneva.

"Reckon so. Man's gotta know his own mind," said Tripper.

Dante said, "Immortal Man, my story is complete. The others must return that we may begin the new chapter."

"Then let us commence. You will go back one at a time."

Meredith stepped forward, holding Beth's hand. "You did it, old man. I'm sure we'll talk. Call me."

Then she was gone. She and Beth returned to Limbo, and from there, to Heaven.

Geneva looked at Tripper, and he moved forward. He shook Sylvester's hand. "Y'all got guts, Sylvester. I guess y'all is the greatest proof of anything that there's good in everyone. Maybe y'all can find the good in Adolf." He laughed. "That'll keep y'all busy for centuries."

"I shall endeavor to succeed. I thank you for your aid, Tripper. Fare well."

Then he was gone.

Geneva stepped forward. "You're a fine man, Sylvester."

"You are a fine woman. Trust me, we shall work together again. Have a good life, my dear."

Then she was gone.

Nicole moved forward last. Before she could say anything, Sylvester looked at her and said, "Dear, Tabitha needs a resting place."

Nicole was frightened. He obviously knew *everything*. But he merely shook her hand.

She finally said, "Of course. Thank you."

Then she was gone.

With that, Sylvester clapped his hands. Jagroth appeared above him, and Fred stepped towards him.

"Well, boss, now what?" asked Fred.

Sylvester laughed. "Now we get to work."

"Oh," said Fred, clearly less than thrilled with that answer.

"Oh, not you, Fred. You have a job on Earth."

"Say whatttttttttttttt?"

Then he was gone.

"Abel. Are you present?"

Abel suddenly popped into space before them. "I am, sir."

"I do not expect resistance to the gradual closure of Hell, which will take some time, likely decades, to relocate these souls. At least, that is what I expect."

Jagroth suddenly appeared above them. "Indeed. They must be assigned or somehow healed, otherwise, the soul will wind up in some manner of psychic limbo. Unpleasant."

"I'm glad to help. I've only been in charge here all these years because I was unlucky enough to be the first one here. It's not like I applied for the job," said Abel.

"Hey! Hey, guyyyyyyyyyyyyys!"

They all turned to see a huge, red behemoth with hooves and horns racing at them with a scared look on his face.

Satan.

He stopped before them. "I hear there's a management change. I want to be in on it!"

Sylvester studied him. "May I rely on you?"

"I know everyone who is anyone here. I'm your man."

Sylvester looked at Jagroth. Jagroth said nothing. Sylvester finally said, "Your opinion, Sir Jagroth?"

"Alas, this is a human decision, Immortal Man. You must choose in whom to place your trust."

Sylvester shrugged. Then he stuck out a hand. "Welcome aboard, Satan. I hope you like the benefits package."

Then they both laughed.

Sylvester put a hand around Satan's back and they began walking towards the base of the mountain. "Let's discuss the restructuring and how to deal with some of the bigger problems here."

"I'm all ears. You get me the plan, and I'll make some calls. We'll have this place in working order in no time."

"Perhaps." Sylvester chuckled. "I can see this will be quite an entertaining few decades!"

Chapter Fifteen
Return to Earth

"This is not going to be good," muttered Kress to herself.

About two minutes after returning from Hell, she realized she had a problem. None of them had considered that someone might return ahead of the completion. The idea was they all left together and thus should all return together.

The problem Kress faced was two-fold. First, she had to be very careful to avoid moving and disrupting the spell, which would unleash psychic heat that would incinerate all of them. Second, the comatose state instigated by the spell and lack of having an aura no longer applied, and her body began to resume basic functions. She had to pee, and she was hungry.

Fortunately, she heard a moan just three minutes after she returned and looked around to see Tripper and Geneva waking up.

"Oh, thank God," she said. "I was fucked if you retards didn't wake up."

"Give it a rest, woman, got me a massive headache," muttered Tripper.

What Kress didn't know, because they were laid on the table in a manner than left Sylvester behind her, is that his bed . . . was empty. Geneva, however, noticed this immediately.

"Tripper, I hear you and Kress. Nicole, are you here?"

"Yeah. I'm with the old guy. I have a whopper of a headache."

Geneva snapped, "No one move. Sylvester isn't in his bed."

"Say what?" snapped Kress.

"He's not here," said Geneva.

Nicole turned, for she was on the other side of Sylvester's bed, and said, "Whoa. I can confirm that. Where is he?"

"Back in Hell, a'course," said Tripper. "His body must've been zapped there, or he called it there, or whatever. Question is, what's that mean for us?"

"Being crispy-friend," said Nicole worriedly. "I prefer not to be bacon."

"It shouldn't come to that," said Geneva quickly. "If his disappearance ruptured the spell, we'd be dead already. Obviously, from the side of Hell, this type of channeling spell can be controlled and manipulated. We should just get up."

"What? What if you're wrong?" snapped Kress.

"Geneva's right," said Tripper. "And I got shit to do, like, well, take a shit."

And with that, he stood up.

Kress shut her eyes.

"Ahhhhhhhhhhhh, gettin' old sucks, damn stiff," said Tripper, stretching long and hard.

Nicole and Kress flew off their beds at record speed. Geneva was close behind them. They looked at each other and said, "We made it! We should call Little Jack. He might be alarmed — Sylvester won't register on aural detectors," said Geneva quickly.

"Reckon so," said Tripper, tapping his foot. It had gone to sleep.

Geneva quickly went to the small table in the room on which there was mostly medical equipment, but also a computer terminal with a direct link to Ops.

A thrilled Little Jack responded within seconds. "Geneva! You all made it!"

"Well, almost. Sylvester . . . stayed behind. It was his choice. I'll explain later. Can you drop the defenses so we can get out and come home? After we pee, of course."

Little Jack said, "Hold on, you know we need a good, clear aural scan. Two minutes."

"Of course."

As the scan ran remotely, Geneva said to Tripper, "Sylvester's body is . . . is it gone? I still don't get that."

"Neither do I. Does it matter? He ain't dead. Not in the sense we mean."

"Valid point. I'll think on this," said Geneva.

Nicole was sitting on the edge of the bed, coming to terms with what she had learned about herself. She kept to herself.

Geneva approached her. "I know that was a tough experience. Do you want to talk?"

Nicole shook her head. "I'm fine. I just . . . have stuff to work out."

"I'm always here if you need me. Just call."

"Sure. Sure, thanks," said Nicole politely.

Kress stared at the door. "All I know is if this scan doesn't finish quickly, I'm gonna pee right here on the floor."

Suddenly, Sam Grant appeared on the screen. He wore a yellow and black checkered shirt and looked tired but happy. Geneva yelled, "Sam! Good to see you up and about."

"You as well. I take it from Little Jack that Sylvester didn't return. Is he running Hell?"

"He is." She smiled slyly. "You are a brilliant man, Mr. Grant. You dispatched Hell, gave Sylvester a job, and made sure no one worries about the Horal. What do you do for an encore? Move the Earth off its axis?"

Sam chuckled. "For an encore, I sleep a lot. I'm glad this worked. It had risks, but Jagroth, one of the Horal, was working with me."

Tripper said, "Figures y'all needed me. Yous'n young pups can't get shit done these days. Takes a man of vigor like me to pull this crapola off."

Geneva and Sam both laughed.

Kress snapped form the back of the room, "Are we fucking done here?"

"Yes, Carole. We appreciate your help." Sam unlocked the doors. Kress immediately bolted for the main facility and the restrooms.

"Sam, what do we do now?" asked Geneva as Nicole finally stood up and stretched.

"Resume life, I think. You could all use a vacation. You did all the heavy lifting. I just supplied the plan."

"Sam . . . Meredith was there."

Sam winced. "Tell me about it later, okay?"

"Okay, but it's all good."

"Later," said Sam, simply not emotionally prepared to deal with his late lover's fate at the moment.

Tripper put a hand on Geneva and said, "Reckon we'll head home. What about Kress?"

Sam frowned. "I don't know. Ops has agents in the area, both St. Martin and Oslo, to keep an eye on her. She's been driven to stop the Horal for years now. I don't know what she'll turn to next. But it's not like we can hold her, and I can't justify killing her after she helped us destroy Hell."

"Course not," said Tripper quicky. "Okay."

"I guess just have her sign a release so we won't get sued if there's long-term effects from her trip to Hell and be one with it," said Sam. He yawned. "Oh, Geneva, Medina is finally online. She wants to talk to you. Thanks for your help. We can talk more in a few days."

"Thank you, Sam. You've changed human history."

"By next week, you'll be bitching I haven't gotten anything done. Later."

Geneva laughed. As she spoke with her sister, Tripper noticed Nicole was moving about.

"Y'all okay, youggin'?"

"I'd like to get home," said Nicole.

"I think we all would."

Kress returned from the bathroom and said, "Well, that part, at least, is easy. I can get us all where we need to go."

Three decades ago, Geraldine Kane was forced out of active duty with Ops due to an injury. She learned patience during that time. She learned more patients during the roughly sixteen months her daughter vanished, hit by a tachyon bombardment by the alien Bule Square, and wound up in Hell with Tripper in 2017.

Despite her worries, she was calmly working on her phone at the kitchen table, which was covered with dinner dishes, mail, and her current kitten, an orange kitten named Sugar. She had just brought Sugar home from the shelter four days ago. Sugar was sitting on Geraldine's coat, which was lay in a ball on the table. Geraldine had a frown on her face, because her update wasn't working.

The wind was strong on this winter night, a storm approaching. This area of Maine was expecting five to seven inches of snow by morning, but it hadn't started yet, and it was already nearly midnight, so it was going to come down hard and fast.

She was listening to Jefferson Starship on a record. She still had records, mostly her father's leftovers, and the record player still worked. The only light was the overhead light for the kitchen. All the other lights in the house were off, other than the night lights. The furnace had been running steadily all day.

"I don't know, Sugar. I think I'm losing this phone."

Sugar gave her a puzzled and disinterested look.

Suddenly, however, Sugar jumped up and ran into the other room.

Geraldine was instantly alert.

Seconds later, there was a flash of yellow, like a yellow egg, appeared in the room and disappeared . . . leaving behind her daughter, Geneva.

"Mom!"

"Geneva!"

They hugged, both crying.

"Oh, mom, you wouldn't believe it!" she gushed.

Then she looked around. "Uh, something's wrong."

"Well, you're naked, but I don't know if that's wrong," said Geraldine politely.

Putting her hands over her chest, Geneva grumbled, "Yes, I presume that's Kress' version of a joke."

"Kress."

Ignoring that, Geneva said worriedly, "No, he should be here."

There was suddenly a knock at the door. Geneva raced to it and opened it, revealing the most awkward thing imaginable — Tripper O'Sullivan, naked from head to toe.

Geneva stepped back and started to giggle. Then she laughed whole heartedly.

"What's so funny, Kane?" he muttered, pretending to be offended.

Geraldine bit her lip. "Come in, old friend," she said, leading him inside and shutting the door. Snow blew into the house.

Geneva had collapsed into a chair at the table, laughing uncontrollably.

"Gol' damn, reckon y'all got some nerve, Kane. Just 'cause I got a lotta hair and some wrinkles ain't no reason to act like a dumb schoolgirl. Y'all outghtta look at your own fat butt in the mirror."

This just made Geneva laughed harder.

Geraldine handed him a coat and said, "Here."

Tripper slipped it on. Geneva was laughing so hard she was crying.

Tripper finally shrugged and said, "Awwwwwwww . . . Hell. Y'all got any beer, Geraldine? Saving the world and destroying Hell is thirsty work."

Sipping from her pink water bottle, Nicole stared at the desert before her the next morning. Kress had portaled her to her Hollywood condo, where she spent the night sleeping, eating ice cream, and thinking.

Wired, she had taken a shower and eaten an entire quart of chocolate peanut butter ice cream. Then she laid out her plans.

She left the house around four, knowing the drive would allow time for the sun to rise.

In the desert, she had to rely on photos from the battle with Sunset and Morgana . . . had to rely on the film that never was made, the one where she murdered Tabitha.

There were no longer any markers other than the railroad tracks, but they were distant. She parked her car, took her purse and water bottle, and opened the trunk. Inside was a shovel, which she pulled out. She also brought out a very large pink and black handbag, like a gym bag. It was empty. She brought it with her.

She wore dark blue yoga pants, a gray hoodie, and jogging shoes. Her hair was in a ponytail, a rarity for her. No make-up, and the cold winter morning wind cut at her face. Though the sun was up, it wasn't warm. Nothing could be colder than the desert in a winter morning, for the dry air caused the temperature to drop quickly.

Putting in her pink headphones, she cued up Jim Croce on her music list, then started walking. She was guided by what she had learned in Hell, and fortunately the railroad was still in place.

The location of the filming was a slight dip. It had further dipped due to heavy rain over the winter. The rockslide was still in place burying that section of railroad. But she was going to the right of that and the right of the filming location.

The desert rose slightly in that direction. There was a significant amount of green brush, due to winter rains, and this early it was far too cold for snakes to be out, so she moved quickly. The wind whipped her cruelly.

Reaching the railroad, she marked it off a broken rail. Then she moved three feet. The ground here looked like the ground everywhere else in the desert, but she knew it wasn't.

Her work began. She started digging, but she was also channeling earth, which made it much easier. The risk to just channeling earth and spewing up the earth was losing her objective.

She was far from anywhere and it was early morning, so crows cawed at her. It began to warm up quickly as the sun rose.

Thankfully, no one wandered into the area. She didn't care if she had to explain herself, but frankly it was easier without the interruption.

Her chore took one hour and eighteen minutes. Then she saw a spongy type of white rock . . . and knew she was on target.

Now she moved carefully, like an excavating archeologist. She gently used wind to start to blow dirt out of the hole. This took another seven minutes.

And then she removed the skeleton of Tabitha. She lay where Sunset had buried her in haste back in '17, covering the crime.

She cried once Tabitha's bones were in the sun.

How could she have done this?

Nicole knew her life would never be the same. She wished she had never remembered . . . and yet . . . she had to. She was an incomplete person without this memory, her emotions and ability to change and redeem herself stunted.

But, Lord, it hurt. And the shame . . . the guilt.

Getting herself together, she put Tabitha's skeleton in the gym bag, zipped it up, and carried her back to the car. She left the grave open. No one would care. There was nothing of value there any longer.

Once at the car, Nicole was suddenly exhausted. She just sat there for half an hour, contemplating everything she had learned. The quiet of the desert made her feel like she was the only person in the world.

Finally, she picked up her phone and called the Institute.

"Hi, Nicole!" said Sandy, obviously surprised and pleased.

"I need . . . I need a friend. I have something to do today, but could I have a room there for a night or two?"

Instantly, Sandy said, "Of course. Do you want to talk?"

"Eventually. Thanks. I appreciate it."

"Anything, Nicole. Take care."

Nicole hung up. Then she looked at the bag and said, "I'll take you to a good home. It's the least I can do."

That night, Nicole crept into the quiet cemetery in Lake Forest in Orange County where her parents were buried.

Slowly, she walked through the dark park. She had night goggles, so she had no problems seeing. Her parents were interred in a far corner near a large maple tree.

Nicole gently channeled earth next to her father, opposite her mother. They had polite gravestones. She didn't spend time with them. She didn't like coming here. To her, they weren't here. They were alive in her head, and that's how she preferred to remember them.

Gently, she channeled and removed earth.

Then she put the body and the bag in the hole.

Then she channeled the earth back.

Then she made sure it looked as undisturbed as possible.

Finally, she rose and said, "May God protect your soul, dear one. I'm sorry."

Then she turned and left . . . unaware the perils of her past were *far* from over.

Chapter Sixteen
The Return

On March 12, 2021, Sylvester took charge of Hell and the rest of the Ops team returned.

On March 13 at one in the morning Las Vegas time, two sisters were driving west on interstate 11, returning to Vegas after a few days visiting friends in Flagstaff. Twenty-six-year-old blonde Seka Sandovahl was driving a '10 Subaru WRX that was red with a custom painted white stripe on the side. She loved her car. Riding shotgun was her brunette college roommate and friend, Brenda Siekowicz. They had both been drinking, and they were doing 75 on the sparsely populated interstate that ran only a few miles, the first part of a project to eventually connect Tahoe to Phoenix by interstate —a project *long* overdue in the eyes of anyone who lived in Nevada or Arizona.

As they came around a curve leading away from Hoover dam, on the westbound lanes, a F3500 pickup with a red trailer swerved to avoid a coyote. This dislodged the trailer, which flew across the median like a missile.

Seka started to scream. Being less than sober, she needed a moment to recognize the situation and get the car turned out of the way. She didn't have the time. Brenda never even had a chance to scream. The trailer slammed into the hood of the car, bringing them to an instant stop and crushing both of them.

Or, at least, that's what was *supposed* to happen.

Because slowly, the women awakened. Their injuries were fatal, grotesque, but they somehow managed to get out of the car.

Then they began to heal.

They screamed.

Seka and Brenda died. Their time had passed, their accident fatal. But their bodies still had uses.

"I love Melville's. Coming here always reminds me of our first date," said Ops paranormal agent Joy Delaney around ten that morning, smiling at Little Jack as she ate her chicken strips.

Now twenty-seven-years-old, Joy, while very pretty, wasn't gorgeous. She had a nice round bottom, perky breasts, good legs, and a happy face. Her hair tended to be straight and parted in the middle, and although a natural blonde she often dyed it lighter. Her eyes were a dull blue, her face pretty, though her nose was a little big. Joy was the type of girl that looked good in nice clothes and make-up, looked average without them, and basically was pretty enough that she could get by if she was willing to play to her assets.

Her fiancée, Little Jack McGrath, smiled. He had been the Director of Field Operations until their recent engagement, causing him to step down so he could form his own company, the McGrath Group.

He was a charismatic young man who enhanced that with exceptional politeness and people skills. He got things done, but not in a dictatorial fashion. No, he did it the *right* way.

Now thirty, he had just a hint of a wrinkle around his eyes, but otherwise looked abnormally young. At six feet and two inches tall, he had presence but wasn't overtly big. He sported short blond hair and usually a huge grin. Despite very big ears, he was attractive. His green eyes made him look like a cat.

He dressed very casually and in a very standardized fashion. In public, he almost always wore the same outfit: old jeans, white tennis shoes, a gray dress shirt with white vertical stripes, no tie, and always the top button unfastened. He wore the same outfit the way Superman wore the same crime-fighting costume.

Little Jack and his late sister, Sherry, grew up together. They were born to Big Jack McGrath and his first wife, Danielle. Little Jack came in 1990, Sherry in 1991. Big Jack McGrath was a legend in both business and the TM business, but a serious back injury in '85 forced him to retire to the purely fiscal end of the TM business. A wizard with real estate and mining, he was worth several billion dollars. Danielle was his acolyte before she became his wife, and she died in a battle with the Head in late 1991, just months after giving birth to Sherry.

Lisa was his half-sister, and they didn't meet until she was fifteen, but he always accepted her as a full sister, showing the hospitality and family loyalty his father had engrained in him. Little Jack learned everything about TM and business from his father. He idolized him, and when his father died in 2012 from brain cancer, Little Jack came to realize it was up to him to carry on the family name.

As for Lisa and Sherry, well, they were incestuous, but everyone had flaws. The one drawback to being incredibly rich, incredibly invested in torture magic, and incredibly powerful was isolation. They had no peers and had turned to each other in a very intimate manner.

But Little Jack's obsession for the perfect deal and his interest in TM led him to conspire with the late Gary Hart, founder of the International News Network (INN), Dr. Robert Kosar, and serial killer TM Marc Bundy to attempt to open a portal to restore the first torture magicians, Elkrod and Quafara, to Earth and under their control.

The result was catastrophic. All six conspirators died when Ops broke up the attempt to open the portal. Little Jack was infused with a dramatic mix of tachyons, portal energy, and psychic heat. Driven insane, he instinctively portaled and was found wandering aimlessly in Detroit a few days later by Ops.[6]

Sylvester Starnes, the Immortal Man and head of Special Operations, drew the power out of Little Jack, restoring him to normalcy. But Little Jack's time had dramatically changed him. He had

------

[6] As outlined in TM series two

seen all times and dimensions simultaneously, but jumbled, like plays in a football game in the wrong order. But what was clear was his destiny if he did *not* change his ways. Moreover, he was the one hope of redemption for his siters, who were in Hell. He had to change to save them, save himself, and save millions — and he did. His sincerity was confirmed by a mental scan by telepath Mary Richardson. Then he took over leadership of field operations in early 2018.

"I'm starting to realize we have a lot of work to do to get married and create our company," said Joy.

"Me, too," said Little Jack. He rubbed his forehead. "But nothing worthwhile is easy."

"Other than sex," said Joy with a laugh.

He laughed at that as well.

Located a few miles from the Special Operations' Vegas headquarters, Melville's was the preferred restaurant of the team. It was in a shopping area off North Lamb, in a small mall that had an O'Reilly Auto Parts store, a Panda Express, and a Subway, all just across the street from a giant Home Depot. The restaurant had no windows and only a small sign in the parking lot.

The restaurant was named after the owner, a former Special Operations paranormal who had been injured in '94 in battle with Kelkirk. Unable to perform, he had retired to open the restaurant. Melville's was probably the finest Italian restaurant in America, but it had a select clientele.

Ops preferred it because they could get a quiet room with a large booth whenever they wanted, which allowed them to talk in private. And obviously, Melville knew the Ops world and their special concerns.

They were at a simple two-person table in the main dining hall, which looked more like an Applebee's than anything else, just with fancy auto racing décor. They were near the door just in case of a need for a quick exit. The parking lot outside as full of cars, and it was busy but not overly noisy.

He nodded. "I can't wait to get away, Joy. But I need to finish the transfer of all the stuff to Medina, make it official, so we can start our new life." He put his hand over hers, her engagement ring sparkling in the light.

Suddenly, Little Jack pulled his hand back and looked . . . stunned.

"What's wrong, baby?" asked Joy with alarm.

He said nothing. He suddenly got up and raced out of the back room where Ops held their dinners, racing into the main restaurant. It was moderately busy. He moved past the island in the middle of the floor where guests registered for a table and headed for the lobby.

Joy threw down her napkin and raced after him, feeling alarm. Little Jack had an incident a few weeks earlier where his id took control of his body, turning him into a monster who tried to strangle her. Ops fixed him, but she certainly didn't want a repeat of that disaster. And given Little Jack's background, well, things like that could happen.

Little Jack raced to the lobby just as two women entered. The two women were unknown at Melville's, but until earlier in the morning they had been known as Seka Sandovahl and Brenda Siekowicz.

All three of them suddenly stopped and stared at each other, being stared at by a waitress and a couple other diners.

"Oh, my God. It *is* you," whispered Little Jack.

Joy arrived . . . just as Little Jack moved forward and hugged the woman on the left, the blonde.

"It's us," said the brunette with a sly smile.

Joy stood, stunned, wondering why her fiancée was hugging these strange and beautiful women. Jealousy raised its head very quickly.

Then Little Jack turned to the brunette. "I knew it would happen! But *how* did it happen?"

The blonde said, "Our assignment in Hell. We redeemed ourselves, took advantage of the chance you gave us." She shrugged. "We were sent into these bodies after a car crash. We used TM to heal the bodies. The souls had already left."

Suddenly, Joy realized who they were.

Lisa and Sherry McGrath.

The *late* Lisa and Sherry McGrath!

Little Jack was crying. So were the women. Little Jack finally said, "C'mon, let's go in back, no need to give the locals a show."

Joy grabbed Little Jack. "Is it *really* them?"

He nodded and kissed her, then said, "I recognized their auras immediately. Those aren't their bodies, though they're close, and yes, it's them." He pinged her nose. "See, this is the bit I was waiting for, why I formed the McGrath Group. They're the new partners I mentioned."

"You . . . you knew they'd be back?"

"Yes. And I know of all the great things to come." He kissed her. "C'mon, let's celebrate."

Joy was stunned as she followed them back, Little Jack, wrapping his arms around his sister's waists. Lisa was on the left, Sherry on the right. As they passed Melville, who was watching carefully as he, being a retired agent, was well aware of the dangers of the paranormal, Little Jack smiled and said, "It's okay, bud. These are my sisters in from, uh, Europe."

"Certainly. Would they like a menu?"

"Nah, just bring us a sausage pizza, large, and a bottle of champagne."

"Very good, Mr. McGrath," said Melville with a wry smile, twirling his handlebar mustache.

When they reached the room, they sat, overjoyed. Joy was perplexed, but happy because Little Jack was so happy.

Lisa said, "I'm not thrilled being named Brenda."

"Hey, our last names are the real problems," said Sherry.

Little Jack laughed. Joy didn't. She looked confused and a little angry. Little Jack put a hand on her arm and said, "Honey, what's wrong?"

"They . . . I mean, those girls are dead? I don't understand this at all."

Sherry said, "Ah, it's okay. We didn't kill them. Now that we're back on Earth, well, like your fiancée here, we are here to do good deeds."

Lisa and Sherry clinked the champagne glasses.

Little Jack smiled and said to Joy, "Sorry, I've been involved in the paranormal so long I forget stuff like this is weird. It's reincarnation. See, anyone coming out of Hell takes over a body — you know, like Quafara did with Kathie Vasquez or Elkrod did with Doc Voodoo."

"Oh, like Andrea Voodoo taking over June Bowman?" asked Joy, recognizing that event from '17. It was just prior to her manifestation and discovery by Ops, and thus something the others were, at the time, still talking about quite a bit.

"Yeah, yeah. Now, souls can sometimes get redeemed from Hell. Usually they go to Heaven, but sometimes those with paranormal abilities can pull the soul back to Earth. Or sometimes, part of the redemption is fixing past mistakes."

"That's us," said Lisa with a wry smile.

"Oh, I see," said Joy.

Little Jack turned to Sherry. "So, who did you take over?"

"College roommates now working the Strip coming home from Arizona. They were drunk, so when a trailer flew at them from the other side of the 11, they didn't dodge in time," said Lisa with a shrug.

"How did you explain the survival?"

Lisa and Sherry looked at each other. "Well, we didn't really have to. The other driver was knocked out. We just got out and were fine." "They had no families," said Sherry quickly. "That's part of the resurrection. Anyhow, we'll take care of closing their old lives and opening new ones."

"Yeah, I'm not going to be Brenda the rest of my life," said Lisa firmly. "Hey, uh, we just got here. Have you seen our buddy yet?"

Suspiciously, Little Jack glared at them. "Buddy?"

"Uh, yeah. Look, he's . . . ah, I bet he's, uh, out back. He was . . . redeemed, too. Sort of. I mean, he's here to . . . I don't know the details, but kind of monitor," said Sherry.

Still glaring, Little Jack asked, "Monitoring for who?"

"Sylvester, I'd guess. But he is on his own sort of redemption mission. But he can't come inside," said Lisa quickly.

"You're talking too fast, half-sis, and that means you're not telling the whole truth. It always did, and a new body doesn't change that," said Little Jack, grinning but in a cold way.

"Let's go out back to the parking lot."

"Okay."

They rose. Little Jack let Melville know they'd be right back, that they just wanted to check out Joy's car. Once in the parking lot, which was really just sixteen free standing spaces wedged between the restaurant and an alley, they saw a shocking sight.

Before them stood an emperor penguin.

Not just any emperor penguin. This one was much taller than average. The average emperor penguin stood a shade under four feet. This one was about five and one half. He was the size of a small man.

And he stood like it. His flippers were on his sides like arms on hips, and he was tapping his webbed foot.

On seeing the McGraths, he immediately snapped, "Jesus fucking Christ, it's about time. It's hotter than Hell out here, and I'd know. And can I say how nice it is to be able to say Jesus Christ again, no matter what the cause?"

Lisa laughed and Sherry hugged him.

"Who the fuck are you?" asked Little Jack, and he looked as bewildered as Joy had in the restaurant when Lisa and Sherry arrived. He was shaking his head, arms folded over his chest.

"Fred. Fred Zarkowitzipzickh33. Yeah, I'm an emperor penguin, but a big-ass one. I busted outta the zoo. And before you ask a bunch of stupid fucking questions, animals have souls, we can go to Hell, I went to Hell, I got redeemed, and I'm here to make up for my sins and help you out."

"What sins are those? Eating too much fish?" asked Joy with a giggle.

Fred snapped, "Hey, bimbo-bitch, I was the first serial killer in penguin history. I gutted forty-seven females. You wanna be forty-eight?"

Joy took a step back. Lisa stepped forward.

"Fred, that attitude will get you right back in the bile pits!" snapped Lisa. "Think it through!"

Fred sighed and calmed down. "Sorry. Old habits die hard, especially in this fucking heat. What is it, like 101?"

"It's like 80, dude. It's a great day in Vegas terms. Well, we better get your ass over to Ops and outta the public view."

"Ah, this is Vegas. Just tell 'em I'm a midget in a costume and it's no problem," said Fred.

Little Jack laughed. "Man, I can see working with you is going to be quite a trip!"

Joy said, "I still don't get the resurrection thing! How come you didn't come back as, I don't know, a plumber or something." She pointed at Fred.

"I came back as a penguin in the zoo that was dying. Anyhow, once I got outta the zoo, I hitched a ride on a supply truck and headed this way."

Joy glared at him. "I don't like you."

"I don't like you either."

Little Jack stepped between them. "Guys, we're all gonna get along, because we've got great things to do. Tell you what, Fred, you come hang with us."

"They got fish here?"

"All you can eat."

"I'm in. For good fish, I'll pretend I'm a midget in a costume."

Little Jack laughed. Joy forced a laugh. As they reentered the restaurant, he took her hand.

"Joy, it will be okay. You're my wife, and no matter what, I'm here for you."

He kissed her.

And she melted in his arms like a romance heroine.